# OKLAHOMA MOONSHINE

## THE MCINTYRE MEN
### BOOK TWO

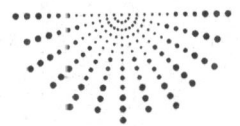

## MAGGIE SHAYNE

OLIVERHEBERBOOKS

Copyright 2016 by Margaret S. Lewis

Edited by Jena O'Connor, Practical Proofing

Published by Oliver-Heber Books

0 9 8 7 6 5 4 3 2 1

❀ Created with Vellum

# CHAPTER ONE

*R*obert McIntyre found the strawberry blonde of his dreams out behind the Long Branch Saloon, near the trash cans. She was bending at the waist and twisting sideways, using her cell phone's glow to try to see the back of her left thigh and holding her skirt up high in the effort. As a result, he could see the full length of her long leg from the shapely calf emerging from the top of her cowgirl boot to sexy curve of her thigh.

He stopped looking by sheer force of will, cleared his throat and said,

"Can I uh, help you with something?"

She straightened, gasped, dropped the skirt and damn near jumped out of it all at once. He held up both hands, "Easy, I'm just one of the owners, taking out the trash." He held up his plastic bag as if to prove it, and reminded himself that she wasn't the woman of his dreams. He didn't dream about women. He had nightmares about them.

She blinked at him for a second, then smiled, patting her chest with her hand. "You scared me half outta my boots."

He was getting sucked into that big white smile, so he lowered his head as if to inspect said boots as he carried the overstuffed bag to the trash can nearest her, took off the lid and dropped it inside.

Cowgirl boots, they were. Brown leather with pink embroidery and heels that would challenge a tightrope walker.

"I was s'posed to meet an old friend here for a nightcap," she said. "But I guess she's not coming. I walked around back looking for a few more bars on my phone, and caught my skirt on a branch. I think a thorn got my leg."

For some reason, every bit of it seemed false, and alarm bells sounded in his head. "You uh—need me to check for you?"

Her brows rose high over those big, innocent eyes. In the overhead lamplight, he thought he saw freckles across the bridge of her nose.

"Are you flirting with me?"

He blinked. "I don't think so. But if you're here for that nightcap, we're closed."

"Oh." She lowered her head. Wavy ribbons of pale honey and sunshine fell down over her cheek.

"I'm the only one here. Otherwise I'd invite you in."

"I don't mind that you're the only one here," she said, real fast and eager. And she beamed those eyes at him, all full of hope. "I mean, you're one of the McIntyres, aren't you?"

"Rob," he said nodding.

"Kiley," she said, extending a hand.

He took it. She had a nice hand, soft and warm, and she gripped his all snug and strong. She had an honest handshake. That was a good sign, right?

"Everyone knows you McIntyres are upright citizens. I'm not scared to be alone with you. And I sure could use that nightcap."

He had no freaking idea why he was grinning like a friendly

chimp, and he quickly tried to press his mouth into a straight line. "Come on in. I could use one, too." Stupid, stupid, stupid, his brain said. He extended an elbow and she grabbed onto it, walking close enough that her perfume made his brain go fuzzy. Maybe not so stupid, he thought.

They crossed the brand new deck, and he opened the door for her, then watched her as she sashayed on through, her skirt swaying, her boots tapping the floor. The big lights were all turned off, but there were night lights on. They were spaced evenly at floor level throughout every room at the Long Branch. As they walked through the kitchen, the counters and dangling pots and pans, and giant cook surfaces and sinks and coolers were all easy to distinguish. "This way," he said, guiding her toward the big double doors, then through them into the barroom.

It was dimmer there, and all the chairs had been tipped up on top of the tables. He walked her right up to the bar, and she slid onto a saddle shaped stool, sidesaddle style.

Rob went behind the bar. "What can I get you?"

"Rum and Coke. Helps me sleep."

He made her a drink, grabbed himself a long neck, and stayed on his own side of the bar. "You don't sleep well, huh?"

"Not tonight. Tonight my dream is circling the drain." She held up her glass. "Here's to believing in last minute miracles."

He tapped her glass with the top of his brown bottle and took a nice long pull from it.

She looked around the bar, pointed at the giant cardboard sign near the jukebox and said, "I've been seeing signs like that all over town. What's it about?"

The cardboard thermometer measured dollars instead of degrees. It was painted red all the way from $0 to $275,000, but the word "goal" was way up at the $500,000 mark. She read the lines across the top aloud. "'Big Falls' Big Future?'"

"People are worried about drought," he explained. "It's been bad south of here, and forecasters say it's coming our way, sooner or later. So the town's raising funds to buy some property and build a reservoir. The land's for sale at three-hundred and fifty, and the rest is to get the building underway."

"I wouldn't have thought a small town like this would be able to raise so much."

"I'm surprised too. The church is giving half its bingo proceeds, firemen are holding chili socials. Every business in town is chipping in what they can. When anyone buys property here, the Post Office automatically sends them a flyer asking for a contribution. Even little kids are selling lemonade for the cause."

"That's nice, everyone pulling together like that." Except she was frowning at that sign like she wished she could see through it.

"It's that kind of town."

"Yeah. Yeah, it is, isn't it?" She studied her drink, turning the glass slowly on its coaster. "I grew up here. Well, 'til I was twelve anyway. Long time ago. I didn't realize how much I missed it until I got back here."

He nodded slow. "Big Falls has a way of getting inside a person. I never intended to stay here either. But now...." He shrugged, deciding not to go on, or he'd start sounding like he believed the local tales about a town that chose its residents and refused to let them go. "You gonna tell me about this dream of yours that's in danger of imminent demise?"

She smiled at him. He thought there should have been a ricochet sound effect to go with that smile when she aimed it his way.

"What is it about sitting at a bar that makes people want to whine about their troubles to the guy on the other side?"

"I don't know, hon, but there's no point bucking tradition, is there?" He found a clean bowl, scooped it full of bar mix from the canister, and set it in front of her. "Whine away."

She smiled at him. "You're a nice guy, aren't you?"

"No. I'm brooding and grouchy. Ask my brothers."

"I will." She pinched a pretzel out of the bowl, ate it, sighed. "You know the old Kellogg place, out on Pine Road?"

"Hell yeah, I know it." In fact, he'd been out there earlier in the week, looking at the ranch with Betty Lou Jennings, Big Falls' resident gossip queen and only real estate agent. The Kellogg property was a thousand acres of prime ground; lush meadows with the Cimarron River running right through it, three ponds, and a hundred-acre woodlot, two barns and a sweet little farmhouse, all about to be auctioned off for back taxes.

"Beautiful, isn't it?" she asked. And she tipped her head sideways and gazed off into space, like she was seeing it in her mind's eye. "That old-fashioned farmhouse with the flower boxes in front, and those shutters with the heart shaped cutouts in them, and the way the porch wraps around one side...."

In his mind, those heart shaped cutouts in the shutters were gonna be the first things to go. He didn't bother telling her so, but he had a feeling a strawberry blond storm cloud was about to start raining on his plans. And when she spoke again, it did.

"I was planning to buy it. They're auctioning it off tomorrow, you know."

"Yeah. I know." He was planning to bid on it himself, on his own, not with the trust fund his father had set up for each of his sons, funds so big they were snowballing under the momentum of their own interest and dividends now.

He wanted to buy the ranch with his own money. Not his father's and not some bank's. He'd saved up enough, and he was about 99% sure the old Kellogg place was gonna be the one.

It wasn't in his nature to bid against a beautiful dreamer. But business was business.

"I don't have enough, though," she went on. "Half, maybe." She turned her dewy glass on its coaster, back and forth, back and forth. "Grandma's sending me her heirloom ring, she says it's worth a fortune. There's a jeweler in Tucker Lake who says if the stones are genuine, he'll buy it. But if it doesn't get here by tomorrow morning, before auction time, I'm doomed." She held up her glass, and said, "Here's to the US Postal Service. May it deliver."

"Here, here," he said. But something had changed in her voice and demeanor when she'd started talking about her grandma's ring. Something that told him she was lying, and he couldn't quite figure out why. It was in the way her eyes shifted away when his tried to lock on, and the softer tone.

She took a long sip from her glass, seemed to really relish it, smacked her lips and closed her eyes, and then set the glass down again. "You probably think it's stupid for a woman alone to think she could manage a thousand acres."

"I don't think it's stupid at all. It's a beautiful spread." He gave in to his worse judgment and came out from behind the bar, slid up onto a stool beside her. He could smell her perfume and feel the warmth of her body sort of reaching out to tease his. But he reminded himself that his track record with dishonest women wasn't exactly stellar. "I'm curious though, what would you do with it? Run beefers?"

"I don't want to raise cattle. I've got other things in mind."

He lifted his brows. "What other things?"

"Lambs and bunnies in the spring—for pets, not for eating. An acre-wide patch of shamrock and clover with miniature leprechauns peeking out here and there for St. Patrick's Day, and four-leaf clovers and pots of gold foiled chocolate hidden for kids to find. I'll host the biggest Easter egg hunt in seven counties at Easter time. I want to try to grow Christmas trees, acres of 'em, so kids can come and pick their own right out of the field. We'll take 'em around on a wagon, or a sleigh those

6

rare seasons when we get a little snow. Maybe have Santa driving it."

"Wow." The way her eyes sparkled while she talked about her plans, the pinkness in her cheeks, those things were damn near taking his breath away.

"I want to landscape the prettiest spot on the place, down by the riverbank, and make it even prettier, then rent it out for folks to hold wedding ceremonies."

"You've really thought this through."

"I've been thinking about it since I was a kid." She lowered her eyes. "I grew up on that ranch. Happier times." She looked up at him and smiled, but it was a sad smile that didn't reach her eyes. "I want to spread my sister's ashes there. But not unless I get the place. If I don't, then... I just want to keep her near me."

And the rainstorm became torrential. How the hell was he going to bid against her now?

"I'm sorry," he said. "Was it recent?"

"Six weeks ago. Almost seven. I don't...I can't—" She held up a hand and her eyes got damp.

Everything in him turned to mush at the sight of those unshed tears. He wanted to chase them away. The power of his attraction to her was shockingly strong. He hadn't felt this drawn to a woman in a long time. Maybe not ever. "Tell me more about your plans for the place."

She sipped her drink, blinked her eyes dry again. "Probably just pipe dreams."

"They don't sound like pipe dreams so far. What about Halloween, what kinds of tricks and treats do you have in mind for Oklahoma Octobers?"

Her whole being shifted, he thought. The light came back into her eyes. "Hayrides and corn mazes and pumpkin patches. The smaller of the two barns would make the most amazing haunted house you ever saw."

"It would, wouldn't it?"

"Mm-hm. I'll name the place Holiday Ranch. It's gonna be a gold mine." She was smiling hugely when she looked his way, then lowered her eyes, her cheeks going pink. "You must think it's a crazy idea."

"I think you might be kind of brilliant."

"Really?" She looked at him as if his answer mattered. "I really want to know. You have a lot more knowledge about business stuff than I do, being the son of RJR McIntyre."

He knew enough about business to be aware that his own dreams for his someday ranch were not likely to be lucrative at all. But he didn't want to do it for the money. "I agree it could be a money maker, after a while. You might be living hand-to-mouth for the first year or two. Might need to grow some sort of crop or lease some of the acreage to a local farmer to help get up on your feet. Might even need to take on a side job until things start rolling. But it's a sound idea. And you're only just scratching the surface of what you can do out there. Gift shop, maybe an on-site coffee and snack bar—"

"Oh, that's good. That's really good." She smiled at him. "Thanks for that. This is important. It's a new beginning for me. A whole new life."

She finished her drink and reached for her handbag.

"Nope. It's on the house."

She smiled up at him, then slid off her stool, landed on the floor, and stumbled a little on those heels. He caught her shoulders and she tipped her head up, met his eyes, and hers turned soft and smoky.

He felt a rush of something warm and dangerous whispering through him. The urge to kiss her was like a giant hand on the back of his head, pushing him closer.

But Rob resisted. "Night, Kiley. It was real nice meeting you."

~

8

Kiley left that fancy saloon like she was walking on a cloud. She was going to do it. The ranch was practically hers!

Rob McIntyre was polite and sweet and charming, and according to that bumblebee-like real estate agent Betty Lou Jennings, who loved to gossip while showing potential buyers like Kiley around properties, he was very interested in buying the old Kellogg place. He'd be at that auction tomorrow for sure. All she had do was get there ahead of him and wait.

He was more handsome than she'd expected. Yes, she'd seen him from a distance, because she'd been researching him. But up close, it was like being pulled by the force of his gravity or something. He had the sweetest face she thought she'd ever seen. Thick, full lips and a wide broad smile that made his eyes crinkle up. Dark hair that wanted to curl, and just enough scruff on his face to send her hormones into overdrive.

He was so over-the-top nice to her that she'd have suspected he was running a con of his own if she didn't know he was rich. Rich folks could afford to be polite and charming for no reason, she guessed. But it would have been easier if he'd been a jerk to her. Or if he looked like an ogre. Or if his smile hadn't just about made her forget how to breathe.

This was gonna be hard. It would work, but she almost wished it didn't have to.

Kiley Kellogg was turning over a new leaf, going straight, creating a respectable life in her small hometown the way she'd always secretly dreamed of doing. Being that her father was in prison and her sister was dead, she didn't think the message could've been any clearer; she needed to change her life if she didn't want to end up like they had.

But going straight required capital, and she only knew one way to make bank. She'd never been worth a damn at it, nowhere near as good as her dad and Kendra. A constant source of disappointment to them both, as a matter of fact. But if she wanted her home back, she was going to have to up her game.

9

She had to con a billionaire cowboy into handing her half a million dollars. And she had to do it in a way he would never suspect had been a con at all, because she wanted to go on living in this town once the ranch was hers again. She might even consider paying him back.

She got into her beaten and barely road-worthy car, and then drove it home. It was all of five minutes if you took your time. Right out of the parking lot of The Long Branch Saloon, two miles down, then right onto Pine Road. The ranch her mother had inherited and her father had pissed away, included both sides of Pine road, a full thousand acres of it, wide flat meadows and scrubby woodlots, generously watered by the Cimarron.

Home.

Her battered car's headlights lit the rutted driveway and picked out what remained of stonework pillars on either side. There used to be a gate attached, but it was long gone. Just the rusted hinges remained, their orange-brown decay staining the stones.

She shut the headlights off before driving on through. It wasn't exactly legal to be squatting on the property before she'd bought it, but she couldn't afford much else. The trip from New York had cleaned out most of her cash. Besides what she'd set aside for the auction.

She had five hundred thousand dollars in cash, stuffed into a duffle bag, crammed behind the wall in the back of a bedroom closet. She and Kendra used to hide their diaries in there.

She pulled all the way up to the house, and then drove around behind it, cut the engine and got out. Then she just stood there for a minute, looking around. The sky was so much wider here than in New York, a blanket of twinkling stars, spread as far as you could even see. No moon tonight, and hardly a cloud, either.

When she was a little girl, she and Kendra used to sneak out on nights like this. They'd wander down to where the river meandered through the meadow, and spin until they were too dizzy to stay upright. Then they'd open their arms and fall backward into the deep grass and wildflowers, giggling until it was hard to breathe. When the laughter ebbed, they'd keep lying there. That was the best part. Lying there in the silence of an Oklahoma night, listening to the bullfrogs and grasshoppers and nightbirds, and gazing up at all those stars. Sometimes a fish would jump and splash in the river, or a bullfrog would croon a baritone lullaby.

It would be good to reclaim her home, to be able to live there legally. Good to turn it into what she and Kendra had talked about as kids.

She felt close to her sister there. Closer than she'd felt to her in years. They'd struggled so hard to stay in touch when their father had gone to prison and they'd gone into the system, moving from one foster home to another, never in the same one together. They'd made sure they never fell out of contact back then.

And then they'd turned eighteen and had been booted out on their own. Kendra wanted to run games, con the wealthy, and get rich quick. Kiley wanted to take classes and learn how to make an honest living, so she only grifted when she had no other choice. They'd run one or two fairly successful games together, but they just didn't see things eye to eye. Kiley felt guilty, which made Kendra feel judged. Angry fights ensued, and they'd drifted apart.

She slid her hand into her big handbag and closed it around the black leather drawstring pouch that held Kendra's ashes. "I've just gotta run this one last game to get the rest of the money for the ranch, Sis. Once it's mine and no one can take it, I'll spread your ashes here. Down by the big boulder on the riverbank."

Guilt gnawed at her belly. It was always the same. If she ran a game and failed, which happened more often than not, she hated herself for not living up to her dad's expectations and her sister's phenomenal skills. If she ran a game and succeeded, she felt even worse.

All those people who'd sent her money through *Go-Fund-Yourself.com* for her non-existent Chihuahua's make-believe prosthetic legs, haunted her dreams at night. It had been the most successful con she'd ever played. And it was still only half enough to buy her home back. To fund her dream.

And that was why she had to go straight. She had never been any good at the game anyway. And if she started to *get* good at it, she thought that would be even worse. She just wasn't cut out to be a criminal.

One more game, and she'd have enough to get her home back. And that was it. No more.

Kiley nodded, affirming to herself that all of her dreams were about to come true, and then she went inside, crawling through the same window she'd been using for the past few nights. The house was empty, but had been spruced up for potential buyers. She trailed her fingertips over the fresh paint as she went upstairs to the bedroom that had been her sister's, walked into the closet and pulled away the board that covered up the hollow spot in the wall. Just inside the dark opening her sleeping bag waited, all neatly rolled up. The smaller green duffle contained most of her worldly possessions. Clothes and toiletries, mainly. The bigger green duffle held the cash. She hauled everything out except the cash, and dropped it all onto the bedroom floor.

Her styrofoam ice chest full of food and bottled water stood in the farthest corner from the bedroom windows. There was no electricity turned on in the place, and it was summer and hotter than hell by day. But the century-old farmhouse stayed remarkably cool. Would stay cooler still once she put some curtains in the windows.

She unrolled her sleeping bag, gave it a shake, in case of visitors, then stripped off her clothes, and crawled inside, tired and lonesome, but closer than ever before to her dreams coming true. She just wanted to snuggle down, close her eyes, and imagine how it was going to be.

So she did.

# CHAPTER TWO

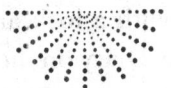

hen Kiley opened her eyes again, smiling lazily and stretching her arms, the sun was way higher than it ought to be, and blazing at the wrong angle through the bedroom window.

"Holy smokes!" She crawled to her clothes, rummaged through them for her cheap cell phone, and flipped it open. Five minutes to nine. The auction was at ten.

There wasn't time for her usual early-morning bath in the river down back. She snatched clothes and makeup bag out of her rucksack, grabbed two bottles of water from the cooler, and ran for the second floor bathroom. Shoving the stopper into the sink, she poured the water into the spotless basin and did a fast wash-up. Face first, body second. Hair...ah, hell, hair.

It was a mess. She pulled a large-tooth comb through her curls, then piled them up on top and snapped a pretty clip into place. Then she slapped on a coat of makeup, and ran back to the bedroom and into the closet for the cash. She unzipped the duffle just to verify it was still there, and she hadn't dreamed it. Stacks of banded bills and a waft of money-smell confirmed that it was indeed for real. She tugged the bag through the opening, and knocked a banded stack off the top of the pile. It tumbled further into the dark compartment.

"Dang! I don't have time for this now." She set the bag aside, and reached way into the opening. The stack of bills was there, on top of something else. Either two bundles had fallen or her money had multiplied overnight.

She pulled both items out into the light. A banded stack of bills, and a small book, with a lock and a tiny keyhole. It was purple with the words My Diary on the front in pink glitter.

Kendra's. Kiley's had been just like it, only pink with purple glitter. She had no idea what had happened to it. But this was definitely Kendra's.

She landed on the floor, on her butt, and held the small book in hands that shook a little. Her throat went tight, and her eyes burned. She could've opened it without the key. Just a solid tug would do it. Or she could pick the lock with a hairpin, if she didn't want to damage the thing.

But instead of doing either of those things, she just sat there, holding that little book in her hands, blinking down at it, trying to keep the hot tears from spilling over and ruining her mascara. "Dammit, Kendra, why did you have to die before we got the chance to make up?"

Sniffling, she put the diary into her purse. "I'm sorry," she whispered. "I'd give anything for another chance to say I love you."

She got to her feet, brushed herself off. The auction would begin in a half hour. She needed to wash her hands one more time and get there before Rob McIntyre. No time to roll up the sleeping bag, repack her dirty clothes, or carry the rucksack and cooler down to the car just then. She left it all just as it was, hefted the money duffle by its shoulder strap, and ran to the car like her feet were on fire.

～

Rob McIntyre was having a mental tug of war inside his own mind. He didn't quite know how he could bid against Kiley Kellogg for her childhood home. That girl seemed to want it way more than he did. But she'd also seemed full of blue mud, as his stepmother Vidalia would say, when she'd been talking about some priceless family heirloom that was going to fund her cause. She was a liar, and a very bad one. And while he couldn't think of a single reason why she would lie to him, a perfect stranger, about some non-existent piece of priceless jewelry, he was sure she had.

He didn't like dishonest women. He'd been badly burned by one, and he'd vowed to live his own life as honestly as possible from then on. He'd given up lies, even little white ones, and it felt good. He was waiting for a woman who was as honest as he was.

But for some reason, he liked Kiley. She was young, early twenties if he had to guess. And maybe he was drawn to her because she was all alone in the world, or maybe because she'd recently lost her sister. He'd seen the truth of that pain in her big topaz-blue eyes. Maybe it was because of the way she lit up when she started describing her plans for the ranch, or maybe it was because those plans were so unusual and creative and intelligent.

Or maybe it was just because she was pretty enough to knock the wind out of him every time she smiled.

He hadn't slept a wink or stopped thinking about Kiley and the ranch all night long.

Knowing he'd see her at the auction gave him some kind of a thrill in the pit of his stomach and a case of the jitters at the same time, and he was pretty sure it also influenced him to put on his brown Stetson at just such an angle, and check himself in the bathroom mirror twice before heading out of his room and down the staircase that spilled into the dining room.

His younger brother Joey was already at a table in the empty dining room, his long legs stretched out from his chair, working on a chest-high stack of flapjacks. "Hey, Rob. Grab a bite before you go? I got more here than I can eat."

"You've got more there than both of us could eat," Rob said, veering off course to head to the table. He didn't sit down, just grabbed a pancake, wrapped it around a sausage and swiped it through the half inch-deep syrup on his kid brother's plate.

Joey lived in one of the rooms above the saloon, same as Rob. Their older brother Jason had bought a run-down place just beyond the west end of town, and was living there while fixing it up. Together with their father, Bobby Joe, they ran The Long Branch Saloon and brought tourists and their dollars into Big Falls.

"You gonna do it?" Joey asked. "Gonna buy that ranch?"

"To tell you the truth, I don't know. I'm a little bit torn." He took a big bite of his hack-job breakfast sandwich and said, "Guess I'll decide when I get there. Wish me luck, little brother."

"I'll do more than that. I'll be there for moral support. I'll be over soon as I finish packing this breakfast away."

"For a normal person, I'd say the auction would be over by then, but for you—I give it ten minutes." Rob shoved the other half of his breakfast-roll-up into his mouth, then headed out to his big red pickup truck.

He drove into town with only fifteen minutes to spare, sticking to the speed limit over Main Street, though it killed him, then finally speeding up at the far end of the village. He was almost to the firehouse where the auction was being held, when he caught a glimpse of something in his periphery and then heard a big *thunk* on the passenger side fender.

He stomped the brakes so damn hard his body lurched forward. The seatbelt would've bruised him, if he'd remembered to buckle it. Slamming the shift into park, he dove out of the truck with his heart hammering, dreading to see what he'd hit.

Kiley Kellogg was just pushing herself up onto her hands

and knees on the pavement. Her palms were scraped, and her eyes were tear-filled. "What the—" Then she looked up. "*You?*"

"Are you okay?" He reached down to help her up, and wished his heart wasn't pounding a mile a minute. "I didn't see you! Are you all right?"

"I'm okay, I'm just—" She patted herself down, then widened her eyes, and looked around as if on the verge of panic. "No, no, no. Oh, *no!*" She turned in a slow circle, then started pawing through the grass along the side of the road. "Oh, no, please, not now, not when I'm so close!" she cried.

"Kiley?"

She kept searching until he caught hold of her shoulders and made her stop, raising her gently up onto her feet again. "What are you looking for?"

"The ring!" She wasn't looking him in the eyes, but still scanning the ground. "My grandmother's ring. It must have flown out of my hand!" She pulled free of him and started looking again. "Oh my God, there's a drain! What if it went down there?"

"Then you're not gonna find it in time for the auction," he said. "Not sure how you were gonna sell it in Tucker Lake and get back here with the funds in time either, but—"

"The jeweler's meeting me here with a cashier's check. Oh my God, what am I gonna do?"

Then she went silent for a minute and looked at him. "Wait a minute, why are you here? Are you here for the auction?"

"I uh...was interested in the ranch too," he admitted. Even though he had a pretty strong hunch she already knew that.

"You didn't tell me that last night."

"Seeing how bad you wanted it, I was reconsidering."

She lowered her head. "That was sweet of you, but now it's over. Without that ring, I can't afford it. Unless...I mean, would you...could you...maybe...loan me the money?"

"Loan you the money," he repeated.

She shifted her gaze, lower and to the left. "You *did* hit me with your truck. I mean, look at me. You made me lose my grandmother's ring."

"I did, huh?"

She pulled out her phone. "Call the jeweler in Tucker Lake. Go ahead, it's Skilman's. He'll tell you what he offered for it based on the pictures I sent him, providing the stones were real, which he was going to verify when he got here."

Rob had no doubt the jeweler would do just that. But he wasn't just handing her five hundred thousand dollars based on photos she'd sent to a jeweler. She could've got photos of a priceless ring off the internet, for crying out loud. He wasn't an idiot.

And in that very moment, it became clear to him why she'd told him about the ring in the first place. To set him up.

And yet, he couldn't quite bring himself to call her on her bullshit and walk away. There was so much hope, so much need in her eyes. And there was also a pretty significant chance he was jumping to the wrong conclusions based on his history, painting her with the old Paula brush. Probably not, but it was possible.

"How old are you, Kiley?" He blurted the question without thinking first, and knew it was rude as hell. But once it was out, it was out.

She blinked. "I thought cowboys were polite."

"I'm only an aspiring cowboy." He stood there, watching her and waiting.

She gnawed her lower lip, didn't meet his eyes. "Twenty-three. What does that have to do with anything?"

It had a lot to do with everything, he thought. She was young. She was trying to con him, and she was terrible at it. But she was also beautiful, and heartbroken, apparently all alone in the world and desperate to reclaim her childhood home. Something about that just grabbed hold of his heart and twisted.

He was pretty sure he was about to do something really stupid. But everything in him was telling him it was the right move. He probably should have taken time to mull on it some, but there wasn't really any time to take.

"I'm not gonna loan you the money," he said.

"But—"

"But I *am* gonna help you."

Her frown got even deeper. "Help me how?"

She sounded like she was accusing *him* of being up to no good. He thought it over for a long minute, waiting for the voice of reason to kick in and outshout his impulsive decision, but he found himself counting those freckles across her nose instead of counting the ways this could go terribly wrong.

"The auction's gonna start any minute, Rob McIntyre, so if you have some magic way to save me without giving me the money you just cost me, then spit it out."

He figured he'd probably kick himself later. "You said you have enough for half, right?"

"If it doesn't go for more than I think it will."

He nodded. "Okay then. We buy it together. We go in as partners." He watched her face.

She seemed to be casting around inside her brain for some kind of counter offer. Then someone stepped into the open firehouse doorway and called, "Auction begins in ten minutes!"

Kiley sent a desperate look skyward, chewing her bottom lip and getting teary eyed.

"My operation wouldn't interfere with yours at all," he said.

"I don't even know what your operation is."

"Horses. Quarter horses. I want to breed them, raise them, train them. There's plenty of acreage for both. I'll use the bigger barn for stables. You want the little one anyway. We could do this." Then he shrugged. "But I get to live in the house. For now, at least."

"But...we don't even know each other."

21

"It's that or nothing," he said.

"But...my grandmother's ring!"

"Yeah, too bad about that," he said. "Tell you what—if you find it, you can buy me out."

"But...but that's not fair."

"Seems fair to me." People were filing into the firehouse, taking up their seats. "Look, I'm just gonna go on inside now, get a good spot up near the front. I can buy the whole place myself. I don't need a partner. If you're not interested, I'll just—"

"All right, all right!" she said quickly. "Okay. I'm in."

"And I get to live in the house?"

"Yes, yes, yes." She extended a hand his way. "Deal."

He shook her hand, then said, "I've got to get the truck out of the road."

"I need to find a restroom and clean up," she said, looking at her scraped palms. "Meet you inside."

When Kiley Kellogg walked into the crowded firehouse, every head turned, Rob's included. Not only was she new in town, and therefore a subject of great interest to the locals, but she was also beautiful in a fresh-faced, innocent way that made you want to trust her.

If she could lie without it showing in every cell of her body, Rob thought, she'd be dangerous.

Joey, who had arrived and found him while Kiley had been freshening up, said, "Hubba, hubba! Who is that pretty little thing?"

"That's my new business partner. We're going halves on the ranch."

Joey's eyebrows reached for the sky. "For real? Since when? I just saw you twenty minutes ago, and you said—"

"I know what I said. Things changed. I think she's looking

for me. Come on, I'll introduce you. Uh, soon as you roll up your tongue, close your mouth and wipe the drool off your chin."

Joey blinked and looked his older brother's way. "Oh, yeah. Sorry." Then he grinned. "You calling dibs, though? 'Cause if you're not—"

"I'm calling off limits," Rob told him. "If I'm gonna be in business with her, I don't need that kind of complication, Joe. Sorry."

He started meandering through the crowd toward Kiley. She spotted him, smiled brightly and he tripped over the floor. Those eyes of hers, so blue you could paint the sky with them, had the impact of a wrecking ball when they locked onto his. No wonder Joey'd reacted the way he had.

With his brother on his heels, he made his way through the crowd to where she stood. She had a white paper Big Falls Pharmacy bag sticking up out of her purse. "Did I miss anything?" she asked.

"Not a thing," Rob told her. "Kiley, this is my brother, Joey. Joe, Kiley Kellogg."

"Kellogg? Like in 'the old Kellogg place'?" Joey asked, offering his hand.

She took it and shook once, smiling. "I wish I could say, 'as in heiress to the Frosted Flakes fortune,' but no, you got it right. I lived there as a kid. Just never got the place out of my system."

Joey's smile widened. He liked her, Rob could tell. And what was not to like? She was a charmer.

There was a vat of coffee on a long folding table on one side of the room, and people were constantly making their way to or from it. It was surrounded by styrofoam cups and several cream and sugar bowls. There was one of those Big Falls' Big Future fundraising signs right beside the table, with a plastic cylinder for donations, already half filled with bills. The remainder of the table was taken up by a wide selection of pastries. A Sunny's

Bakery sign was taped to the wall behind them, and there were stacks of flyers and cupcake shaped magnets with the bakery's phone number on them, taking up the two inches between the edge of the pastry trays and the edge of the table.

Smart businesswoman, that Sunny.

The auctioneer took to the front of the room, and people began to quiet down. "I think it's best you do the bidding for both of us, Rob," Kiley whispered.

"Why's that?" Joey asked before Rob could respond.

She smiled. "Because the locals will realize that it's a lost cause trying outbid a McIntyre."

Rob frowned, not the least bit comfortable with that. He hadn't thought of it before, or he'd have got someone to come in and bid on his behalf, just to keep things fair and upright. He was big on fair and upright. They were part and parcel of honesty. And honesty had been his thing ever since Paula...but he wasn't going to think about that just now.

"Look we're gonna get the place either way, right?" Kiley asked, looking up and directly into his eyes, resting one hand on his chest right where his heart started beating faster. "So why should we pay more than we have to?"

"She has a point," Joey said.

Kiley sent Joey her laser beam smile. "Of course I do. When you grow up poor, you learn to find advantages where you can. It's not the kind of thing I expect a man like you to understand, Rob, but maybe you could just trust me on this? Just this once?" Someone bumped her, or something, because she stumbled closer, her chest pressing against his for a second, and her other hand closed on his shoulder to hold on, as she cast an irritated look behind her.

Rob didn't see anyone back there, though. And she didn't move away, despite the fact that there was room to.

"Besides," she said, her breath sweet and minty. "If I'm wrong, then people will bid anyway. No harm done."

"All right," he said, fully aware that his brain had shut down and his mouth was on auto-pilot. "I'll do the bidding. But you'd best not take this as a sure thing, Kiley. I don't want you all disappointed if we don't get the place."

"You're so sweet," she said.

Then she stepped away from him, removed her small warm hands from his body, and took a careful look at the people around them, her eyes turning sharp and interested. "Do you know if anyone else plans to bid on the place?" she asked.

He looked around too. "Most of these folks are locals. Probably just here out of curiosity."

"And for the free goodies," Joey put in. "But hey, that guy's new, front row, left of center. You know him, Rob?"

Rob looked where Joey was focused and spotted the stranger, a short man, heavyset, with male pattern baldness ringed by super dark hair. He wore an expensive suit and was sipping coffee from a foam mug.

"Never saw him before."

"He's a lawyer," Kiley said. Her tone had an edge to it that he hadn't heard before. Not so much sweet southern twang anymore.

Both guys shot her a look and Rob asked, "You know him?"

"Nope. But I can smell 'em a mile away. He's here to bid for some client or other. I'm gonna keep track of him."

Before Rob could reply, Kiley was moving away from him, weaving her way to the front of the room toward the stranger, and the next thing he knew she was squeezing herself right in beside the man.

The stranger shot an irritated look her way, and she beamed up at him, blinking those baby blues and saying something to him.

The guy smiled at her, almost visibly melting.

Joey elbowed him. "Holy crap, those eyes of hers oughtta be

certified as deadly weapons." Then he frowned, and shot his brother a look. "What do you know about her, anyway?"

"Not a damn thing," Rob said. "Just met her last night."

"And you're gonna go into business with her? Robby, are you sure this is a good idea?"

It was seeming like less of a good idea with every minute that passed, but the auctioneer banged his gavel, and the Kellogg ranch was the first order of business. Within a few seconds, that lawyer standing beside Kiley Kellogg was raising his paddle. Every time Rob bid, the stranger bid a little bit higher. Three others started bidding too, but as the price went up, they dropped out one by one.

Rob knew they were getting close to Kiley's maximum. The alleged lawyer was looking down at a cell phone every few seconds, probably texting with his client, and it didn't look as if he'd got the "quit" message yet.

And then Kiley looked down, which made Rob look down too. In between elbows and arms, he saw her rummaging around in that white pharmacy bag of hers.

"What the hell is she—"

Joey elbowed him. "Rob, it's your turn. Bid or you're gonna lose it." Distracted, he raised his paddle, and the auctioneer recognized him and kept on barking. When he looked up again, Kiley was glancing back at him, and she flashed him a thumbs-up sign.

What the hell did that mean?

He looked at the man who stood on her right, sipping coffee from his white foam cup while looking down at his phone screen. Nodding, the fellow raised his paddle once more.

The bidding went on, back and forth, just between the two of them, three more increments up. Rob was raising the price by smaller and smaller amounts, which probably signaled to the other fellow that he was getting close to his limit. The guy smelled blood. He wouldn't quit.

And then suddenly, the fellow spun around and shouldered his way to the aisle. Once clear of the bystanders he broke into a run, disappearing into the hallway where the restrooms were.

"This is it!" Joey said, and he grabbed Rob's wrist and lifted it, paddle and all.

The auctioneer accepted his bid, then asked for others, but of course there was no one there to give them. Bert, the auctioneer, glanced down at Kiley, and said, "Is he coming back, ma'am?"

"I surely don't know," she said. "He muttered, 'too rich for my blood' and then ran outta here like the devil was on his tail."

The auctioneer shrugged and said, "Going once, going twice," and then he banged the gavel. "Sold!"

"Holy shit," Rob said.

Joey clapped him on the back, grinning, then he hugged him full on. "Congratulations, Rob! You did it! You got your ranch."

Kiley sent him a gorgeous, innocent smile, and sauntered toward the exits, shoving her little white drugstore bag further down into her purse on the way.

Rob wasn't entirely sure, but he thought maybe he'd just made a deal with the devil.

# CHAPTER THREE

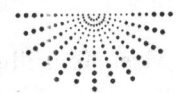

*A*n hour later, Kiley was in the fire chief's office, which had been commandeered for concluding auction business. Four folding chairs surrounded the chief's desk, all but two of them occupied. A handsome man sat behind the desk, but he got up, smiling when Rob walked in.

"Congratulations on the ranch," he said, coming around the desk to shake his hand and clap him on the back. "I think you made a really good purchase today."

"Thanks Cal. Meet my new business partner. Kiley Kellogg, this is Caleb Montgomery," he said. "Local lawyer and my step-brother-in-law. If that's a thing."

"Business partner?" Caleb looked surprised.

Kiley dropped her big duffle bag onto the floor beside her to free up her hands, then shook Cal's. He was looking at her in a friendly, but extremely curious sort of way, and then back at Rob.

The two women in the folding chairs stood as well, looking like opposite ends of the same coin, one, a stranger to her, was tall, painfully thin, with black and silver hair cut very short. The

29

other was the short, round, bubbly Realtor, who wore her bright red hair in a shoulder length, Texas Big sort of style.

Rob continued with the introductions. "This is Mrs. Terwilliger, Big Falls Bank and Trust," he said, introducing the thin one. "And I think you already know Betty Lou Jennings."

"I do," Kiley said. "Hello again, Betty Lou."

"Hello, Kiley. I'm so glad this worked out for you two." She smiled as if she meant it.

"Nice to meet you, Mrs. Terwilliger," Kiley said to the banker, but that lady didn't crack a smile.

They all took their seats, Rob pulling his folding chair up close to the desk.

"First things first," Caleb said, "Do you have the payment?"

"I came prepared," Rob said, and he handed over a certified check for his share. He'd run across the street to the bank while other items were being auctioned.

"Me, too." Kiley, the only one still standing, hefted her duffle bag up onto the desk and unzipped it.

Blinking at the bag full of banded bills, then at Kiley, Mrs. Terwilliger arched her brows over her silver rimmed specs. "*Cash?*"

Kiley blinked at her. "Cash is still legal tender in Big Falls, isn't it?"

"Certainly, I just....just a moment. I'll be right back." She crossed the office and left the room.

"Gee, she acts like she's scared of it or something," Kiley said. There was a warble in her voice, and she bit her lip. Wouldn't do to show nerves. But she sure didn't need people poking around trying to figure out where she'd got all that cash.

"She's probably not used to seeing that much money all stacked up in one place. Then again, who is?"

"Bankers are, that's who." But she smiled at him, regaining her sense of elation. Her dream was coming true after all. Well, sort of. She hadn't dreamed about a partner, other than her twin sister.

Mrs. Terwilliger came back in with the auctioneer, Bert Rowe, right behind her. Dour-faced, she returned to her chair, and nodded at the duffle on the desk. "Mr. Rowe is going to count the cash and sign off on the amount, Miss Kellogg. And then I'll ask Mr. Montgomery to do the same. This protects both of us from any...."

"Shenanigans?" Kiley asked with a smile.

Betty Lou giggled and said. "That's as good a term as any. I'll count it, too, if you all want." Her voice was as high and happy as a bluebird's song.

"Even better," Mrs. Terwilliger said as Bert took the duffle off to one side of the room and began to count out the stacks.

While he did that, Caleb shoved documents at them, and they both signed several of them. Betty Lou, who informed Kiley proudly that she was not only Big Falls' one and only Realtor, but also the town's one and only public notary, witnessed their signatures and certified them with her handy little notary stamp.

Finally, all was said and done and they had a receipt and a copy of the deed. "We're sending the paperwork in today," Betty Lou said. "You'll receive a deed with your names as owners just as soon as all the paperwork processes through. As a rule, that should take two weeks. If it goes longer, you call me and I'll look into it for you."

Kiley lifted her brows. "You will?"

"Sure I will, hon. I help facilitate a lot of these county tax auctions. I'm on a first-name basis with most of the pencil pushers in charge. Oh, almost forgot the best part." She opened a briefcase and pulled out a set of keys for each of them. "Congratulations on your new ranch," she said. Then she quickly yanked two more documents from the case and handed them each one. "I grabbed some Change-of-Address forms from the Post Office, just in case you need 'em."

Kiley stared at Betty Lou and wondered why the woman was being so nice. What did she have to gain from it? Her commission on the sale was already a done deal. She didn't have to do anything extra to earn that. So what was she up to?

Betty Lou Jennings would bear watching, that was for sure.

As they stepped out of the firehouse into the bright, late-morning sun, Rob turned to Kiley and held out a hand. "Congratulations, partner."

"Thanks, partner."

Her small hand was completely enclosed by his bigger one. It gave him a shiver of something sort of primal.

"So...um...are you...heading out to the ranch now?"

She was stammering a little. Maybe the contact was having the same kind of impact on her. "Probably not until morning," he said. "I need to pack up all my stuff. But first I have to break the news to the family. Caleb won't say a thing without asking me first, but that Betty Lou loves to gossip."

"I know she does," she blurted, then sort of gnawed her lip in that way she had, and averted her eyes, and he could hear her unspoken "Oops." She quickly found a new subject. "Your family, huh? You mean your father and your brothers, right? But Joey already knows, he was here."

She was looking around as if she'd only just noticed Joey was missing. Then she spotted him, waiting in his truck. He waved her way, and she waved back.

"My brothers know. I haven't told Dad yet, because that means telling his wife Vidalia, and her five daughters, the youngest of whom is my half-sister Selene, and their five husbands, and—"

"Holy smokes. That's a lot of family."

He nodded and they started walking together back toward his truck, which was parked near his brother's. Both vehicles were tuned up, souped up, lifted up sources of male pride. Joey's was green and Rob's was red. Both were Fords. The McIntyres were a Ford family. "It is," he said. "And there's my mother, down in Texas, and her new husband, too. How about you? Where's your family?"

Smiling, she lowered her head. "Dad's...out of the country. He's a businessman. Kind of an...investment broker. Mom died when I was three."

"I'm sorry to hear that."

She shrugged. "I don't really remember her." Something passed through her eyes, but it was so brief he couldn't tell what it was. It felt awfully sad, though, and awfully big. "Kendra was my only sister." Then she took a deep breath. "Your brother's waiting to congratulate you. And I've got stuff to do, so...."

"Okay." But he didn't turn away. Just kept looking at her, oddly reluctant to leave. "You want to meet me at the ranch tomorrow morning? Take a look around as owners for the first time?"

Her smile returned, brighter than the Oklahoma sun. "You bet I do."

She trotted away from him, around a corner and out of sight. Within a few seconds he heard the sound of a very sick engine coughing to life like a chain smoker first thing in the morning.

Then he headed to Joey and the pickups.

Joey leaned out his open window, and said, "Going back to The Long Branch?"

"Nope. The Corral. Gotta call a family meeting, fill 'em in before the Big Falls grapevine does."

"Good idea. Vidalia's sure to whip up some kind of mouth-watering lunch, or brunch or something."

"You ever think about anything but your belly, kid brother?"

"Rarely, big brother. Rarely."

"I don't know where you put it. Hollow legs, I guess."

Grinning, Joey started his engine. "You might as well send a group text."

The group text feature was overly utilized by the Brand half of the Brand-McIntyre clan and had taken some getting used to. There were three groups. One with the entire family included, one with just the females, and one with just the men, which he still wasn't sure the women knew about. He, his dad and his brothers had been added to the other two groups, and as a result, he'd had to set his phone permanently to vibrate. Otherwise, the chimes would've been as maddening as the bells of Notre Dame had been to Quasimodo.

He pulled out his phone, tapping on the most recent all-inclusive clan text and sent one out. "I have news to share. Can anyone spare a few minutes this afternoon?" he typed.

The replies came so quickly, in such abundance that the phone almost vibrated right out of his hand.

Vidalia Brand-McIntyre's OK Corral didn't open until later, so they had the entire saloon to themselves, and Robert wasn't surprised to see the whole fam-damily had gathered. Vidalia's youngest, Selene, met him at the batwing doors, and clapped an arm right around his shoulders. "We're taking bets," she said, all silvery blond hair and mystical pale blue eyes. "Mom says you've fallen in love. Dad thinks you've decided to move back to Texas."

"And what do you think?"

"I don't think things, I know things." She gave him her most mysterious smile. "And what I know is that you are about to step out of the shadows and into the light."

"That's so vague, it has to be right," Joey said, sending her a teasing look.

She shrugged. "He's becoming his own man. And there's a beautiful stranger helping him do it. Specific enough for you?"

Joey blinked twice and looked at Rob. Rob just shook his head. "How do you do that, Selene?"

She winked, then moved aside to let the rest of the family greet him and try to guess what was up. Vidalia and her first-born, Maya, came out of the kitchen bearing platters stacked with sandwiches, and set them on the table. "Caleb has a lunch meeting with a client, Robby," Maya said. "But he says he already knows your news and he wouldn't give me so much as a hint."

"He's only known for a few hours, if that helps," Rob said.

He looked around at the huge family his father had dragged him and his brothers into. It hadn't been a choice on their part. The Brands were like a Venus fly trap. You got close enough, they just wrapped their sticky arms around you and held on. There wasn't any escaping it. Kind of like Big Falls, itself. And while they seemed overwhelming and meddling at first, once Rob had relaxed into their warmth, he'd found himself wondering how he'd ever got by without it. It was cold out there in the world.

Vidalia's daughter Melusine and her husband Alex Stone were out of town on a job. They were both PIs with their own lucrative agency. The others were all gathered around, taking seats at the table. Maya had her 4-year-old twins with her. Kara and her husband Jimmy, Big Falls chief of police, had brought their son Tyler. Edie and Wade hadn't reproduced yet, and Selene and Corey probably never would.

Rob's father was behind the bar, drawing tall glasses of beer from the taps and lining them up on the bar top. His older brother Jason came in behind him with two giant white sacks bearing the Sunny's Bakery logo on them, and grinning like he'd just won the lottery.

Something was up with Jason. He'd been altogether too happy lately. And if he kept frequenting Sunny's place, he wasn't going to fit his jeans anymore.

Everyone gathered around the pushed-together tables and started passing the food. Vidalia caught Rob's eye and said, "You gonna keep us in suspense 'til dessert, Robby?"

Rob winked at his stepmother and said, "I've done something kind of drastic, and I want you to know before the grapevine gets hold of it."

He had their attention. His dad sipped a beer, but everyone else was quiet, watching him, waiting.

"I bought the old Kellogg Ranch at this morning's tax auction."

"Hot damn! That's a gorgeous spread," Selene said, smiling at him. Her husband Corey nodded his agreement.

"Are you gonna run cattle?" Vidalia asked.

"Horses."

Lots of questions were asked all at once. Rob held up his hands and noticed his father was the only one not animated and inquisitive. "I need to tell you the rest. I took on a partner."

"That's ridiculous, you've got plenty of—"

"I know, Dad. Hear me out on this. I wanted to buy it on my own, without any of your money. I wanted to start from scratch, just to see if I could do it. And I'd saved up enough. But that wouldn't have left me any extra for buying stock and getting the place up and running." He saw the hurt in his father's eyes, and the way Vidalia leaned closer to him, slid an arm around his waist, and said something soft into his ear. He nodded, but he still looked wounded.

Rob went on. "Then I met someone who also wanted to buy the place, and only had about enough for half. So we threw in together. She wants to—"

"She?" Vidlalia's head came up, and her eyes sparked with interest.

Selene said, "Mysterious stranger. Told you so. She's beautiful, too, right?"

"Who is she?" Maya asked. "Someone local?"

"Her name is Kiley."

"Wait, wait, you don't mean Kiley Kellogg?" Vidalia asked.

"Yes, Kiley Kellogg. She grew up there." It was really tough to get a word in with the way his family loved to interrupt. "She's got this plan to use part of the land to do holiday-themed stuff for kids. Hayrides and pumpkin patches, corn mazes and a Christmas tree lot. I figure there's plenty of acreage to do both. I agreed to let her name the place Holiday Ranch, and she agreed to let me live in the house."

Vidalia was frowning, the wheels behind her eyes turning.

Maya said, "When do we get to meet her, Robby?" She was always friendly, supportive and strong, the heir apparent to the matriarchy of the Brand-McIntyre clan.

"I thought I should tell you first. She's got no family, other than a businessman father who's out of the country, and frankly, I think she could use one."

"Businessman father," Vidalia muttered.

Maya sent her a look, then exchanged one with Selene, Edie, and Kara. The Brand women tended to speak without words all the time. It was damn uncomfortable for the men of the tribe, who never seemed to learn the unspoken language of the women. Rob thought maybe the women liked it that way.

"So you're moving out of your room above The Long Branch?" Jason asked. He'd already moved out himself. His fixer-upper outside of town had once been a blacksmith's forge. That left Joey as the only owner still occupying one of the six guest rooms on the second floor of the saloon.

Bobby Joe said, "I wish you'd have come to me first, son. I

may not know much about ranching, but I know about business."

"Believe me, Dad, I'm gonna have plenty of questions about running a business before long. And there's no one else I'd want to ask."

His father nodded, but still seemed less than excited for his middle son.

Then Jason broke the tension by saying, "I haven't seen you this animated about anything since you came here from Texas, Rob. And I'll tell you what, anything that shakes you out of that morose state you've been in this past year and a half is something I'm for."

He nodded, then said, "It's like the dark shell I've been wearing just cracked and fell away."

"That's what it seems like, looking at you," Joey said. "But I'm not sure it was the ranch that cracked you."

He sent Joey a "shut-the-hell-up" look, then got back on topic. "I'm gonna head out there in the morning. Got a few calls to make today. Get the electric turned on, stuff like that. But I knew there'd be talk around town, and I wanted to tell you first." He glanced his dad's way. "We're gonna need to hire more help at the saloon, Dad. I'll try to keep up until we can find someone, but—"

"There are enough of us to pitch in 'til we find a new hand," Maya said. "Shoot, I can sling drinks with a twin on each hip when the chips are down."

He didn't doubt it one bit, although her twins were too big to need carrying on her hips anymore. "Thanks, Maya."

Vidalia snapped her fingers. "There were *two* Kellogg girls. Twins. Kiley and….another K name. Kelly?"

"Kendra," Rob said, but his heart had contracted at the rest of her revelation. "She died recently, Kiley said. She didn't tell me they were twins."

All the suspicion left Vidalia's eyes, and she lowered them

and whispered, "Oh, that poor child." She reached across the table and closed her hand over Rob's. "Then you're right to help her. That is what you're doing. Don't try to say different. You McIntyre boys have your father's big, soft heart. You just be careful Robby. The way I remember it, the Kelloggs were... " She stopped there, searched for the word, and finally settled on, "...troubled."

He didn't like the sounds of that, but he wasn't going to ask for more. A year and a half ago, before coming to Big Falls to be with his father when they'd all thought the man was dying, Rob had made a conscious decision to be completely honest with everyone in his life and to involve himself only with people who could return that honesty. To him that meant not prying or snooping or gossiping to find out about Kiley Kellogg. The honest way was to simply ask her.

Kara said, "You know that place is gonna need a good scrubbing before you can move in." She wiggled her eyebrows and looked around the table at her sisters.

Edie picked up on her message. "And furniture. And dishes. And towels and bedding," she added.

"And pizza and beer," Selene put in, elbowing Joey and grinning as he nodded in wholehearted agreement with her.

Vidalia nodded. "Fortunately, we've done this sort of thing before. No point waiting for morning, either. I have a friend at the power company and she'll switch you on like that," she said with a snap of her fingers. "So we can get started tonight. We'll meet you out there around seven, Robby. Don't you worry. You'll be right at home in no time."

"I um—wasn't worried."

39

# CHAPTER FOUR

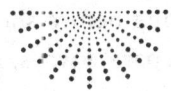

*T*he big boulder was right where it had always been on the bank of the Cimarron River. She was sitting on top of the rock where she'd been for hours. She and Kendra used to jump off into the river. There was a nice deep spot, perfect for swimming, that you could hit if you pushed off hard enough.

Somehow, they had managed to hit that deep spot every time. Never once had they landed short and broken a leg in the shallows. How they'd done that was beyond her, because it looked almost impossible from her grown-up perspective. They just hadn't known any better, she guessed.

She was glad Robert wouldn't be coming tonight. She wanted one more night alone here. And this night was perfect.

The sun had gone down, and the sky was starting to come alive with stars, a handful at a time. As she sat there on top of the boulder, hugging her knees to her chest, a lone bullfrog croaked once or twice. And then another one joined in, and then some crickets started chirping along. It got noisier as it got darker. And when the fireflies came out, it was purely magical.

She reached into her coat pocket for the leather pouch she'd been carrying with her ever since she'd left the city. There was a plastic bag inside, and inside that, were Kendra's ashes. Holding the leather in her palms, she said, "We were supposed to do this together. We were gonna come down here and pool our funds and buy our home back. We vowed it when they took us away and Daddy went to prison. Remember? I don't know how you could leave me like you did."

Kendra had left her long before she'd died. They'd left each other, really, gone their separate ways, fallen out of touch. Kiley hadn't heard from her in a year, when she got the news of her sister's death along with her ashes, by mail.

"I'm gonna live a good life, Kendra. The kind of life we'd have had if Mom had lived. And I'm gonna do it for both of us."

She looked at the pouch, thought about opening it, tearing the plastic and pouring her sister's ashes out right there in the place where they'd been happiest. But something stopped her. Doubt, that's what it was. Doubt that this whole thing was gonna work out for her. Doubt she'd get to stay. Doubt that she even had it in her to make an honest living and not have to con people to get by. If it all fell apart and she had to go, it would be easier if she could take Kendra with her.

Nodding, she tucked the pouch back into her jacket pocket. Maybe she'd just give it a few days or even a few weeks. Make sure this dream come true was for real, and sustainable, before she committed. After all, her plans had not included a partner. A co-owner.

"There you are."

She turned and saw Rob McIntyre standing in the wild-flowers a few feet away. She hadn't heard him coming. The river was far enough from the house that she hadn't even heard his truck arrive. "Oh, hey. I thought you were waiting for tomorrow."

"I planned to." He lowered his head, smiled. "I guess I was too excited to wait. Same for you?"

"Yeah." She slid down off the boulder, landed in the grass, started toward him. "You been in the house, already?" She thought about her clothes and sleeping bag and all her other stuff, still in the upstairs bedroom just as she'd left them this morning. She'd expected to have more time to get her things out of there.

"Yeah, briefly, looking for you. I didn't get far though. My uh...my family is here. Part of it anyway."

"Your family?" His great big, giant-sized family? She lifted her eyebrows.

"Apparently there's a tradition of swarming new homes with buckets and mops and pizza and beer."

Her lips pulled into an involuntary smile. "Pizza and beer sounds good." She sighed, took his arm, turned him around, and started back across the meadow. "They're at the house now?"

"Vidalia and two of the girls are. Kara and Selene. I'm told more are on their way."

She'd been thinking she'd have to tell him tomorrow that she had nowhere to stay. She hadn't quite perfected the story as to why, or what had happened to her former living arrangements. His family being there was actually good. It would give her more time to come up with a believable tale.

"They must be really nice." She tried to remember if she'd known any of the Brands during her childhood. She was sure her father had—he'd known everyone in Big Falls. But she couldn't remember Vidalia or any school friends by the name of Brand. If the sisters were all Rob's age or older, then they were older than her. Maybe she'd missed them all.

Besides, they wouldn't be apt to recognize her, not after all these years.

But what if they did? And what if Vidalia knew her father had been a con-man who'd left a lot of angry residents behind? And what if she knew he'd ended up in prison, and that she and Kendra had finished out their childhoods in foster care and grown up to be as crooked as their father before them?

"Are you okay, Kiley?"

She looked up at him quickly. "Yeah, why?"

"You looked a little sad when I first came out, is all."

"Deep in thought. Not sad. Just imagining all my dreams for this place. And you know... I did have a few problems crop up today. Nothing I can't handle though."

"Anything I can help with?"

She smiled up at him. "I'll let you know." Then she pointed. "Oh my gosh, look, more of your crew have shown up."

The house was in sight now. Another truck had pulled in, and his brothers were piling out of it. She recognized Joey, and could tell even from a distance that the other one must be Jason. God, was every male in the McIntyre line gifted with leading-man genes? They looked it. A mini-van was right behind the truck, and two women got out of that one. No one was empty handed. One was blond and carrying a stack of familiar flat boxes.

"Is that the pizza you mentioned?" Kiley asked.

"Looks like."

She smiled. "Hot damn. I think I'm gonna like your family, Rob."

Kiley wasn't used to this sort of...involvement was the best word, she supposed. She'd have called it meddling, except that Rob didn't seem to mind his entire family showing up to clean his house without being asked. For her, it felt like an invasion of privacy. But she couldn't very well say so. None of them, including Rob, knew she'd been staying there.

At least, not until Selene with her impossible corn-silk hair and glacial blue eyes, said, "Robby, it looks like someone's been squatting in one of the upstairs bedrooms."

Kiley averted her gaze. They were all sitting outside on pickup tailgates and front steps, eating their pizza while fireflies danced to the country music wafting from the radio. They'd been cleaning for a while already, and she hadn't had a chance to slip upstairs yet.

Rob asked, "Really?"

"Yeah, there's a sleeping bag and some food up there. I left it alone, in case it was one of yours."

Rob was looking at her. Kiley could feel his eyes on her. So she said, "I'll go take a look," and dropping her pizza slice onto a paper plate, she got off the top step where she'd been sitting and hurried inside, through the kitchen to the living room and up the stairs.

She paused at the top to push a hand through her hair. Dammit, she should've moved her stuff. She'd overslept, then had to rush to get to the auction, then returned all eager to talk to Kendra, and maybe spread her ashes down by the river, and kind of got lost in her memories down there. But she should've moved her stuff first. Practical matters came before emotional nonsense. Practical matters included keeping her cover intact. These people had to believe she was the woman she was pretending to be. The starry-eyed, innocent but ambitious entrepreneur with a slight crush on her business partner. The nostalgic local girl, reclaiming her childhood home. She could never let them see the real her. A penniless con artist sleeping wherever she could find a spot, while trying to figure out a way to con Rob out of his half of the ranch.

Because that was what she had to do. Clearly. Gaming him out of enough cash to pay for this place was supposed to have been her last con ever. She'd really meant it when she'd told herself it would be. But she'd never intended to take on a partner who owned half the place. This was *her* home.

So one more con might just be necessary, and that was a shame, because she was starting to really *like* the guy.

Still, she had to outsmart them all. Her cunning was her only advantage here.

She took a deep breath and walked down the hall and into the bedroom. Her sleeping bag lay unrolled on the floor, the clothes she'd worn yesterday right on top of it. Her toothbrush was visible in the still unzipped makeup bag, and her cooler sat beside the rest.

She sat down on top of the cooler and let her head fall into her hands. Her father would be ashamed of her, making such a rookie mistake.

"So you've been staying here," Rob said from the doorway.

Looking up quickly, she met his eyes, read them, saw that he wasn't just guessing. He knew. "How do you know it's my stuff? Could be anyone's."

He smiled a little. "Well, I'm a guy. A guy's not gonna forget an outfit like that. At least not within twenty-four hours." He nodded at the rumpled white top and ruffly skirt as he said it. "Besides, the upstairs bathroom smells like your perfume. And also, you didn't even look in any of the other rooms. You came straight to this one."

"Didn't know I was under surveillance," she said.

He frowned, his big brows bending as he studied her. "You weren't. I don't believe in that kind of thing. I came upstairs 30 seconds behind you to check out the alleged squatter. I wasn't trying to be sneaky."

She sighed, lowering her eyes, looking for a believable story to spin for him.

"You don't have to lie to me, Kiley. I'm not gonna judge you."

She brought her head up slowly. "I'm not a liar."

"Good. I'm glad, because I really believe in honesty. It's a big deal to me."

"To me too." She bit her lip, because she'd just lied to him again, and she hadn't even meant to.

"You spent every penny you had on your share of this place. You don't have anywhere else to stay. Am I close?"

She didn't know how to respond. Honesty did not come naturally to her. It felt too close to vulnerability. "It's only a temporary thing. I've got funds on the way, I uh, just...there was a delay, and I haven't got a bank account set up here, yet, and—"

"You have nowhere else to stay."

"Not at the moment."

"But you never mentioned that when you told me I could live in the house."

She shrugged. "I never said you could live here *alone*."

He pursed his lips, nodded slowly. "So you're nitpicking words when we both know what you implied, what I understood? Come on, Kiley, you're too good for that." He came further into the room, handed her the paper plate that held her untouched slice of pizza. "It's gonna get cold," he said. Then he manifested two long-necked brown bottles from the back of his jeans, and handed her one of those, as well.

She took it. "Thanks. And...I'm sorry." She took a big bite of pizza, and it was delicious, so she took another. Then she twisted the cap off the bottle, and washed the bite down with a swig of beer. "This is good," she said, looking at the label.

"Algernon West. It's a little microbrewery out in Tucker Lake. The locals love it." He took a swig of his own. "So what are we gonna do about this?"

"I don't know. I really thought I'd have options, but...." She trailed off there, because he was looking at her like he knew she was lying. He was good. How did he do that?

"You have an idea, though," he said. "You've known you had nowhere to go a lot longer than I have, so you've had time to think on it. Come on, tell me. How was this all playing out in your mind?"

She blinked three times, and couldn't find a lie that would make a bit of difference to him. He'd rocked her, knocked her off her game. No one had ever done that before. No one other than Kendra.

Kendra was so good. So much better at the game than Kiley was. She could fool Kiley almost every time when they were kids. But Kiley had never once fooled Kendra.

"Don't try to come up with a plausible story, just tell me the truth," he said, watching her face like a hawk watches a mouse. "Try it and see what happens. I dare you."

She frowned. Just telling the truth and seeing what happened had never even occurred to her. The Kellogg girls had been raised to never tell the truth unless they couldn't come up with a lie that sounded better and would elicit sympathy for their cause, whatever that cause happened to be.

Telling the truth just because he asked...wow, was that how normal people really lived?

He was looking at her face, his eyes kind of roaming it all over, and nodding encouragement at her. Sighing, she said, "I guess I was thinking we could try living together. I mean, not *living together*," she added rapidly, "Just...sharing the house. It's big enough. Four bedrooms, two bathrooms, and if we shared living expenses we'd both have more extra money to put into the ranch." She bit her lip. "Not that money's an issue for you."

"It is, actually. I want to do this on my own, with money I've earned, not the family fortune. I'd just as soon add to it as I go along, then leave it all for my kids."

"You have kids?" she asked, stunned.

He smiled, shook his head. "No. But I might someday."

She did not understand him. He had a fortune he didn't want to spend. He wanted to make it bigger so he could give it away to kids that didn't even exist yet. She didn't think she'd ever met anyone like this guy. He was completely crazy.

He came further into the room and sat down on her sleeping

bag, reached up to take a couple of potato chips from her plate. "So like I told you before, honesty is important to me. I decided about a year ago to tell the truth all the time."

"Got lied to, huh?" she asked, taking a seat beside him. He shot her a surprised look and she shrugged. "Was it a woman?"

"It was."

"She break your heart?"

He pressed his lips, then said, "Cracked it pretty badly. Hurt my pride a lot. But mostly I just felt like an idiot for falling for her game."

She'd never thought about that before, about people who bought into a game feeling stupid afterward.

"Kiley, I can't be in business, much less share a house, with someone I can't trust."

"That's kind of a stupid rule, Rob."

His brows went up. "Why's that?"

"Because everyone is out for themselves in this world. You're better off not trusting anyone, ever. People are always gonna do what's best for them, and if it hurts someone else, too bad."

"Every man for himself, huh?"

"And every woman."

He nodded. "Well, I guess we're gonna have to agree to disagree about that philosophy. But as to the rest...I meant what I said. I can't be in business with someone I can't trust."

"Well, how do I make you trust me?" she asked.

"By being honest."

"Well, how do I know I can trust you?"

He studied her, nodding slowly. "Good point. Okay, how about this? We both agree, here and now, that we'll always do what's best for the ranch. That way, you can feel comfortable that you know my motives well enough to be honest with me. Do you think you can do that?"

She thought for a second, then lied. "I can if you can."

MAGGIE SHAYNE

"Good," he said. "So I'm gonna ask you a question. And I'd like you to answer me honestly."

"Are you *testing* me?" She was starting to get pissed. How dare he?

"No. I don't play games like that. I just have a simple question. Remember that guy who was bidding against us at the auction?"

"Sure I do." She looked around the bedroom. Where the hell was her purse?

"Did you put something in his coffee?" Rob asked.

It was in the car, that's where her purse was. In the car, and the car was unlocked, and he'd probably looked inside it, given that he'd already admitted he didn't trust her as far as he could throw her. So he knew. He *was* testing her. The rich, arrogant bastard.

"Kiley?"

She slugged back more of the beer, swallowed hard. "Ipecac," she said. "A few drops of ipecac. It's harmless, they give it to toddlers to make 'em yak up stuff they shouldn't have eaten. Poison berries and what not. He had to go puke, and we got our ranch. No harm done."

He looked at her like he'd never seen her before, blinked as if in shock, got up and turned toward the door.

"Oh come on, Rob." She jumped to her feet, too. "We would've lost the place if I hadn't—"

"Just because you're gonna lose doesn't mean you get to cheat," he said.

"Cheat my Oklahoman ass. Where is the law that says you can't make a guy puke to get what you want?"

"I'm pretty sure it's called assault."

"*Assault?* He threw up. I didn't *hurt* him. God, why are you being so dramatic?"

He kept walking. She raced after him. "You told me to be honest. You said you wouldn't judge me. Who's the liar now,

50

Rob? You're just a pampered, rich son of a gun who's always been able to buy anything he wants. You've got no clue what it's like to be denied, to have to struggle, to not know where your next meal is coming from, to have nothing to your name but a POS car held together with chewing gum and twine, and not even know where you're gonna sleep from one night to the next, and—"

"Okay, okay." He put his hands up like she'd pulled a gun on him, then turned slowly, and lowered them again. "You're right, I was judging you. And you're also right that I don't know what your life has been like. I'm sorry." He sighed. "Thank you for being honest with me about the...ipecac."

He had cut her off just as she was working up to a great rant. It was frustrating. *He* was frustrating. "You're...welcome. I guess."

"I can't move back into my room over the saloon. Jason's already rented it out. So I guess we'll have to try this your way."

She blinked in shock. "You mean...share the house?"

"Yeah. I mean share the house." He nodded past her, at the room she'd just exited. "I take it you'd like this to be your room?"

She nodded.

"Okay." He turned away again, then paused at the top of the stairs. "How much exploring have you done since you've been back? You look in the barns yet?"

She shook her head. "The barns are probably still packed full of junk, both of them. Been that way for as long as I can remember. When we were kids, Dad forbade us from going anywhere near them. We did anyway, but..." She stopped there. "Why do you ask?"

"There's an old car out in the big barn. God only knows if it's salvageable, but I think it's in better shape than the one you're driving. Edie's husband Wade owns the garage in town. I'll ask him to give it the once-over. No labor charge for family. Just parts, and he might be able to find used ones or salvaged ones and make it work."

"But...I'm not family," she said.

"I am. You're my business partner, so that's close enough."

He continued down the stairs.

Kiley tipped her head to one side and watched him go. His long legs and easy stride, his broad shoulders in that denim shirt, and the dark curly hair that tickled onto his neck and probably needed a trim.

He was not for real. He could not possibly be what he was trying to convince her he was. Captain America. An overgrown Boy Scout. The last honest man on planet Earth. He couldn't be that.

Which only meant one thing. He was trying to con her. And since the only thing she had of value was her half of this ranch, that must be what he was after.

But no. He could've bought it on his own. He had plenty of money. He didn't have to partner up with her. So if he was after anything, it wasn't the ranch.

Her eyes widened. Maybe he just wanted to get her in the sack. Could that be it? Were rich people so stupid about money that they'd spend half a million just to get girl into bed?

Probably.

No. She didn't think that was it, either.

It occurred to her that he might just be a nice, honest, decent man. She didn't really think there were such things, but if there were, they would probably be in Big Falls, Oklahoma. Maybe he was the last of a dying breed?

Nah.

# CHAPTER FIVE

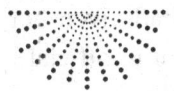

*T*he night was lit by a billion twinkling stars, a million blinking fireflies, and three sets of fading red tail-lights as the Brand-McIntyre fleet rolled away.

Robert stood in the middle of his living room, which no longer echoed like a cave, because it was full of stuff. Crossing his arms over his chest, he perused the modular sofa that fit the room like it was made to be there. Fawn colored leather, butter soft, and not a hint of wear.

"You're looking at that couch like you're deep in conversation with it." Kiley stepped over the still-rolled-up, braided area rug and dropped onto the couch, bouncing a few times to test it out. She patted the cushions on either side of her. "I think it's awesome. That Edie has taste."

Edie had been the first of Vidalia's daughters to take her aside and say something nice to her. "I heard about your sister. I can't even imagine," she'd said, and she'd glanced past Kiley at her own sisters and her eyes had grown wet. She was beautiful, blond and the most put-together woman Kiley thought she'd ever seen. "If you need anything, just let me know."

She hadn't seemed to have any other motive.

Each of the sisters had done the same at one point or another during the evening of cleaning. Selene had taken hold of her hands and told her Kendra was still with her, and always would be, and she'd given her a little crystal stone she said was supposed to ease the pain of grief. Kara invited her to come by for coffee anytime she needed company. She was home days, running her daycare center and would love the chance to get to know her better. Maya had given her a long hug and told her she would love to have an unofficial little sister to love, and so would the rest of her family.

That one had almost made her cry. She'd never met women like them before.

Rob sighed loudly, snapping her back to the moment. He started to say something, then stopped, and looked at the sofa again.

"What? You don't like it?" she asked.

"I don't *not* like it, it's just...."

"Oh." She nodded knowingly. "It's used," she said. "And you're not used to sitting on other folks' castoffs."

"Don't make it sound like I'm a snob."

"That's kind of the definition of a snob," she said.

"What, that I've never owned used furniture before?" He shook his head in denial. "No. That doesn't make me a snob."

She patted the spot beside her. "Prove it." And when he hesitated, she added, "Come on, Rob. Edie said she had it cleaned just before she put it in storage. And if you ask me, she probably had plastic over it before then. That woman is *flawless*."

"She used to be a model," he said. "And just so you know, in Brand lexicon, 'storage' means Vidalia's barn." Still, he crossed the room and sat down on the sofa beside her. It stretched out five feet or more in either direction, curving into a lazy L.

"They really came through for us. Well, for you, I guess. Since they don't know I'm shacking up with you yet."

"They know."

She blinked and sat up straighter. "Aw, come on, you didn't tell them I had nowhere else to go, did you?"

He was still leaning back on the sofa. "I told you I wouldn't tell anyone that."

"I know you did. So did you tell them anyway?"

He frowned at her. "No. I told them we're gonna share the house and see how it goes. I don't make promises and not keep them, Kiley. I don't say things I don't mean."

She looked at him hard, tipping her head to one side. "Not ever?"

"Not ever."

She pondered that for a moment. Then she straightened her head and nodded hard. "Suppose someone asked you if their jeans made their ass look fat. And suppose that those jeans did, in fact, expand their already massive backside to mammoth proportions. What then?"

"I'd look at their soul. And I'd tell them they were beautiful."

"Oh my God. I think I might just puke."

He laughed.

"Don't laugh at me."

"I can't help it. You're so damn cute. Twenty-three and making me feel every bit of my own thirty-two years."

"Oh, yeah. You're ancient," she said.

His laughter died, but the killer smile remained. He looked at her as if he really enjoyed looking at her. "Will you tell me about yourself?"

She sighed and thought for a second, searching her mind for an answer, trying to spin one from whole cloth. Then he said, "Will you tell me something *true* about yourself?"

"Still harping on the truth thing, are you?" she asked, but she said it real softly.

"I just went into business with a girl I've known for about a day. Yeah, I'm harping on the truth thing." He shrugged. "It's important to me. It wasn't always, but it's who I am now."

Taking a slow inhale, she nodded, thinking hard. "I miss my sister."

Her answer took him by surprise, she thought. "Hell, Kiley, I'm sorry."

"We hadn't seen each other in like a year." She leaned forward, balanced her elbows on her knees, clasped her hands. "We didn't get along once we grew up. But as kids we were *really* close."

"Twins, right?"

She snapped her gaze his way. "How did you know that?"

"Vidalia remembers you as little girls. Said she never knew what happened to you, why you left Big Falls."

He waited, but she didn't volunteer an answer to that. She said, "We were inseparable. We roamed the woods on this place like we were born in a den and raised by coyotes."

"Did it drive your dad crazy?"

"No. He preferred us outside. If he kept us indoors we tended to break things. Oh my God, the day we shot our bb guns in the attic and broke the stained glass window, I thought he'd kill us both." She closed her eyes. "I didn't know it then, but it was my mother's favorite part of the house. I regret breaking it to this day. But back then...hell, we were kids. What did we know?"

She blinked because her eyes were burning, and kept her head down, so her hair was a curtain between them. Then she leaned back again and stared at the empty wall they faced. "We really need a TV."

"A couple of 'em," he said.

"And beds," she added. "That clan of yours didn't bring any beds. But dang, they brought everything but." She looked around the living room. There were boxes everywhere. Dishes, pots and pans, cutlery. There were stacks of bedding, sheets, blankets and comforters and throws. Vidalia had brought enough curtains to cover the windows in a skyscraper. There were two reclining chairs, a rocker, a small round dining table with four wooden chairs, and a stack of towels and washcloths that didn't look as if they'd ever been used. "It's gonna take us a week to unpack it all."

"At least." He looked her way. "You want to take the first shower?"

She grinned at him. "Thought you'd never ask. Selene stocked the bathroom, too. Fancy-stuff. I hope she didn't spend a fortune."

"No, she makes it."

"She makes...what? Shampoo?"

He nodded. "And conditioner and soaps, and herbal teas and ointments and all sorts of brews and potions."

She lifted her brows. "She some kind of a witch?"

"She calls it Wiccan, but yeah."

That made Kiley smile even harder. "You believe in that stuff?"

He thought on it for a minute. "Never have. But I'll tell you one thing, those soaps and things of hers are amazing."

"And you don't think that might be cause she sprinkles a little magic into them?"

He shrugged. "Now that you mention it, she did say a beautiful stranger was coming into my life."

Her smile died and she blinked fast and looked away, pressing a hand to her cheek. It felt hot, like she was blushing. Then she got up, grabbed the big box of towels and other bathroom supplies, and ran upstairs, carrying them with her.

Rob watched her go, then sighed and shook his head. She was something, his new business partner. Conniving, manipulative, and with the moral values of the coyotes she'd mentioned might have raised her, as far as he could tell. He didn't like dishonest people. But he liked Kiley. There was something about her, some kind of innocence underneath the surface.

He'd watched her, watching Vidalia and her daughters all evening long. She studied them the way he figured a novice painter would study Da Vinci. With a mixture of admiration and longing.

He supposed it was a good thing he liked her. He was kind of stuck with her.

No. No he wasn't. He had the family fortune to fall back on. If he wanted her out, he could buy her out. But he didn't think he'd have the heart to do it, so he hoped it never came to that.

This place meant everything to her. He'd known it the minute he'd seen her sitting out there on that boulder, staring at the river like a lost soul staring at the Pearly Gates.

"*Robbeeee!*"

Her shout startled him right out of his chair, and he ran upstairs, thinking she must be facing down a cougar or something, and burst through the bathroom door. She stood there in nothing but one of those brand new towels. At least he thought that's what she was clutching around her. He couldn't tell for sure because his eyeballs couldn't see anything except the parts of her that were *un*covered. Tanned legs, shapely as hell. Toned arms and softly rounded shoulders. There was something delicate about her neck, the place where the collarbones framed the dip in between them. He could see her pulse beating there, soft and rapid, and he closed his eyes in order to re-enable his ability to speak. Belatedly, he said, "What's wrong?"

"Shhh! Listen!" She held up a hand.

Rob listened, and tried opening his eyes while his head was tipped downward, but wound up mesmerized by her little toes. And then he heard it. *Scritch, scritch, scritch.* He looked up. The sound was coming from above them, and he sighed in relief. "That's just something in the attic. A squirrel or a chipmunk. You want me to go chase it off?"

"If you wouldn't mind too much. I have a phobia about rodents."

"Do you?"

"Yes, I do."

"Then I'll go scare him off. But I get the sofa tonight."

"That sofa's big enough for both of us and a guest. But I was gonna take that big brown recliner anyway. Thing's like sitting on a teddy bear."

"Take your shower," he told her. "Relax, I'll deal with the big, scary squirrel."

"My hero." She batted her eyes at him and it made his brain go numb.

Shaking his head to try to reboot his mental functions, he left the bathroom, and she pushed the door closed behind him. But just before it closed all the way, he said, "I wonder where the attic access is?"

"In the closet off the corner bedroom," she said. Then she closed the door. Rob continued down the hall, into the corner bedroom, and crossed to the closet. He went to open the door, but it didn't budge. The wood had swollen a bit. It would shrink back down now that the place was heated, just needed to get the dampness out of the wood, he figured. He yanked harder, then harder still, and the door finally gave. He stumbled onto his ass on the floor when it did, and sat there for a second, blinking and looking up at the square panel in the closet ceiling, and the chain hanging down from it.

He got up and pulled the chain. The trap door came down, and it had a folded-up ladder attached. There was just enough room in the closet to unfold it to the floor. Using his phone as a flashlight, Rob climbed up, brushing cobwebs away from his face as he went in.

The attic bore a layer of dust that made everything in it look ghostly. There were a few boxes, a couple of trunks, a tall oval shape he thought was probably a freestanding mirror, and might be an antique. He walked carefully, watching for weak spots, and finding none. The place was really solid. He clapped his hands. "Gonna have to move along, now, squirrel. This place is spoken for. No more freeloading."

He made a little more racket, but didn't really think he was scaring any critters overly much. He noticed a dusty guitar case beside a box with what looked like books in it, and moved a little closer, crouched low and blew the dust off the top of them. Stacks of tween-targeted paperbacks with bright covers. He thumbed through them a little bit, smiling and imagining Kiley as a happy, wild child. He wondered if Maya would like to keep the books for her little girl to read someday.

Something scrambled across the floor behind him, and he turned, shining his phone's light at it. The squirrel froze, twitched his tail a couple of times, and then scurried up a wall, out through a missing pane of glass in the window. Easy fix.

He went over to check it out. Just an ordinary window that faced the front lawn and driveway. On the floor nearby, though, was a stunning stained glass version, the same size. A few pieces of its colored glass were missing, one of which he knew had been broken by a little girl's errant BB. He pocketed the phone and picked up the window, which was heavier than he'd imagined. It was truly beautiful. And it hit him out of the blue that he could get it repaired and surprise Kiley.

He forgot about the squirrel and the books, and carried his heavy find very carefully back down the folding stairway, which was not easy. Once he got it into the living room, he wrapped it up in one of the donated blankets and carried it out to his truck. He knew a glass repair place in Tucker Lake.

He caught himself thinking of the big reveal, and how thrilled she would be. He pictured her practically bouncing with joy when she saw the window in place for the first time, and caught himself smiling so hard it hurt.

*No*, he told himself. *No, no, no. Don't even start. She's not the girl for you, Robert McIntyre. Not even close. She's confused by the notion of honesty. She poisoned a guy to get this place, don't forget.*

When he came back inside, she was curled up in the brown recliner, wrapped in a blanket, and sipping a cup of hot cocoa. He could smell the chocolate, and the sandalwood scent of one of Selene's herbal shampoos. Kiley had draped a towel between the chair and her head, in deference to her wet hair.

"I made you a cup of cocoa, too," she said. "It's on the kitchen counter."

*She poisoned a guy to get this place, don't forget,* his brain repeated. Unnecessarily. It wasn't like he'd forgotten.

He looked at the mug on the counter, then at her. She blinked her big blue eyes at him.

*She didn't really poison the guy. She just made him puke for a little while. It's not like she killed him or anything.*

He picked up the mug, and she smiled with her full lips and said, "Did you scare away the big bad squirrel?"

"Not only did I scare him away, I found his point of entry and devised a plan to repair it." He tried to think of a reason she might want to make him sick, like that poor slob at the auction, but he couldn't come up with a single one. So he decided to trust her.

As a matter of fact, it felt so good to just decide to trust her that he thought he was going to make it his practice. Just decide to trust her, and give her some time to learn to trust him back, so they could work this place together and make both their dreams come true.

She smiled at him, watching as he sipped his cocoa.

Selene and Edie were having breakfast at the Big Falls Diner, at a table right beside the giant "Big Falls' Big Future" thermometer—the red was almost a third of the way to the top—

when a very large, sandy-haired stranger came in. He swept the interior of the place, the way you do when you're looking for someone. Selene guessed he didn't find them, because he turned his attention to Rosie, who'd hustled behind the counter to wait on him. "Welcome to Big Falls," she said, knowing, just as any local would, that he wasn't from here. "Can I help you?"

He turned his phone her way and said, "I'm looking for this woman. Have you seen her?"

Rosie, whose hair matched her name and always would, thanks to Miss. Clairol, had been running the diner for as long as Selene could remember. Everyone in Big Falls loved Rosie, and Rosie pretty much loved everyone in Big Falls. But she didn't seem too enamored of the stranger just yet.

"I'm Rosie, and I run this place. You are...?"

He seemed to be fighting a giant case of impatience and not winning. "I don't mean to be rude, ma'am, but it's important that I find her and I'm short on time. Do you know her or not?"

"Funny how folks always preface rudeness by saying they don't mean to be rude."

"Do you know her?"

"Can't say that I do."

"You didn't even look at the picture." His voice was taking on a little too much anger, and Selene was on her feet before Edie was. You didn't come to Big Falls and give one of its favorite residents a hard time.

Still Edie managed to get ahead of her before she got to the front counter. They flanked the stranger. "Is there a problem?" Edie asked, her voice soft and charming.

Selene couldn't have cared less about diplomacy. "Yeah, like maybe you have amnesia and forgot what manners are?"

He turned all the way around, putting his back to the counter. "I haven't forgot anything. I'm looking for this girl." He held up the phone. Behind him, Rosie put on her glasses and came around front to look for herself. All three women looked at the photo, then they looked at each other, and then they looked at the man.

They all spoke at once. "Never saw her before."

"No idea."

"Not a clue."

He made a sound halfway between a growl and a sigh, turned, and stomped toward the door.

"Hey, wait," Selene called, pulling out her cell phone.

He looked back and she snapped a pic, smiled and said, "Have a great day, now."

Completely perplexed, he left.

Rosie took off her glasses and let them dangle from the excessively blingy chain around her neck. Selene bet her grand-niece Cora had got it for her. "You girls gonna call your mamma or am I?" she asked.

"I'll put the family on alert, Rosie," Edie said. "Thank you for not saying anything."

"Psssh."

"The big guy really seems to have it out for Kiley, doesn't he?" Selene asked. "His aura is sparking like the fourth of July."

"It's just as well we Big Falls' folk know enough to mind our own business, and stick together when outsiders come snooping around," Rosie said. "I'll see what I can find out about this gent through the grapevine." She lowered her voice to a conspiratorial whisper. "I can put Cora on it. That girl can sniff out truth like a bloodhound."

Selene smiled. "Doesn't even matter that the Brand family PIs are out of town. Thanks, Rosie."

"You think he's dangerous, Selene?" Edie asked.

"He's pissed off, and he's a little bit panicky," she said. "I don't know about dangerous. I didn't get dangerous."

"But pissed off and panicky seems close enough to me," Rosie said, giving them each a long, serious look right in the eye. "You girls be careful."

~

Rob was flipping eggs when his phone made its text sound. The sound he'd chosen for this particular sender was a series of Morse code beeps. The females of the clan had sworn not to text the whole family at once unless it was an emergency. For example, last week's discussion of who was bringing what to Vidalia's Sunday after church meal. That exchange had gone on for forty minutes.

He tipped up the frying pan to slide his perfect eggs onto a waiting english muffin that was already dripping butter and a slice of seriously sharp cheddar cheese. His mouth watered.

"That smells *so* good." Kiley came into the kitchen, carrying her cup of coffee which, she'd told him ten minutes ago, was all she ever consumed in the morning. Her hair looked like the feathers of a very angry chicken.

For some reason, his brain registered her appearance as the sexiest thing he'd ever seen. He was on a slippery slope where Kiley was concerned. It was the damnedest thing, how he'd vowed that he would never, ever, *ever* get involved with a dishonest woman again, and yet here he was, being drawn irresistibly to one.

Something felt hot near his elbow. He jerked it away from the still-blazing burner and remembered what he was doing. Turning off the burner, he set his plate on the little round kitchen table that had probably been in some Brand woman's house at some point in recent history. Then he sat down and picked up his fork.

Kiley came right up to him and looked over his shoulder. "Is that cheese melting out the sides?"

"Yeah. Sharp cheddar. Local, even."

A noisy rumbling sound came from her stomach.

"Excuse me!" she said, pressing a hand to her tummy. "That was rude. Stomach growling like a cougar."

He set his fork down. "You said you weren't hungry."

"Well, yeah, before I saw *that*."

He got up smiling, stepped aside and said, "It's all yours, Kiley."

"Oh, no, no that's not what I was angling for."

"Yes, it is."

"No, it isn't. I'm not gonna eat your breakfast."

"I'm already making another one." The eggs were still on the counter, burner still hot. He turned it back on, set the pan above the flame and cracked two more shells. Then he dropped another muffin into the toaster that somebody had apparently bought brand new just to bring over here last night.

He owed his family big time. The meddling bunch of sweethearts.

"Well...if you're making more anyway," she said, and she sat down.

"I am." His eggs started to sizzle, and he turned to watch as she picked up half a muffin with an egg on top and bit in. Perfectly cooked yellow yolk dripped down her chin. She dragged her forefinger through it and smacked her lips. "Mmm," she said with her mouth full. "*Mmm!*"

"You're welcome. And Kiley, when you want little favors like this, all you have to do is ask. We're partners and we're roomies. Doing nice things for each other oughtta be our norm."

She chewed, washed the bite down with coffee, nodded at him. "So I'm just supposed to walk out here and say, 'That looks great. Would you make me one?' instead of politely waiting for you to offer?"

"Instead of manipulating me into offering. See the difference there?"

She shook her head. "Just seems like bad manners to me. How about I just state here and now that any time you make this particular breakfast, I'm in."

He could not argue with her logic, so he put the eggs away

65

and retrieved the cheese. He was slicing another serving when his text went off again. He'd forgotten all about it.

"All right, all right, just a sec," he told the phone. He put the cheese away, buttered the muffin that had popped up, topped it in cheddar, and flipped his eggs. Kiley watched him the whole time, but looked away when he met her eyes. "What's-a-matter, Kiley? Never see a man cook before?"

"My dad cooked all the time. He just didn't seem to enjoy it like you do."

His senses went on alert. She'd told him precious little about herself, other than her sister's recent death, which was too raw a topic to really try to discuss. He tried to act casual, dropped his eggs onto his muffin, turned off the burner, carried his plate to the table and sat down.

"So your dad did the cooking?" he asked.

She looked up fast, like she had only just realized what she'd said. "Who's texting you?"

"Family."

"They the only ones who ever text you?" she asked.

"No." He tipped his head a little to the left. "Mostly. That particular text tone, though, that's theirs."

She got the joke, and smiled a real smile. "They can probably get to be a lot. I mean, being that there are so many of them."

"They can. I love 'em anyway."

"I could tell last night. Just the way you are with them. And those women. Holy smokes."

"What about them?" he asked.

"They're like...I don't know. Unreal. Smart and kind and gorgeous and...." She tipped her head sideways and said, "They're like what I imagine when I try to remember my mom. And like what I envision when I think about who I want to be."

He was gonna have to remember that compliment and share it with the Brand half of the clan. They would appreciate it. "You close with your family, Kiley?"

66

Her smile turned false. She picked up her second half muffin, took a big bite and shook her head left and right to answer his question without saying a word.

That was okay, he thought. She'd tell him about herself when she was ready. There was no hurry.

Some little voice in his head insisted that there was a hurry. That he was in danger of getting a little bit too fond of her, maybe already was, and she was still keeping a whole lot of secrets. He could see them in her eyes, and everything in him wanted to know everything about her.

He ate in silence for a while, waiting for her to pause between bites, and then he decided it couldn't hurt to try to nudge her just a little bit. "I don't even know where you're from, you realize that?"

"Yes you do," she said. "I'm from here. Oh, hell, look at the time. I gotta run. Busy day!" She got up, took a big gulp of her remaining coffee and ran right out the front door, finger combing her hair on the way.

He'd pushed too hard. Miss Kiley Kellogg was a mystery to him. Maybe that was what was so attractive about her. He'd always had a curious mind.

His phone bleeped. He picked it up this time, frowning to see that Selene had texted him a photo of a WWE wrestler... or someone who looked like one. Frowning, he read the message that followed.

*Dude was just in diner. Flashed pic of Kiley. Asked if we knew her. Rude, impatient, angry.*

A rush of protectiveness pushed him up out of his chair, and his brain went dark and beamed out the message: *That guy gets within a mile of Kiley and I'll kick his oversized ass back where he came from.*

He tried to tell himself it wasn't an overreaction, even though a part of him knew it was.

He was from Texas and he lived in Oklahoma, two places

where it was still okay for men to be protective of women. Besides, she was his business partner, and he hoped, his friend.

Who was he kidding? He hoped for a lot more than friendship.

Her dilapidated car had already gone bounding away down the road, out of sight, and he wished she'd told him where she was going so he could make sure she'd be safe.

He hurried through the rest of his breakfast and threw the dishes into the sink for later attention. It occurred to him that this guy must know something more about Kiley than he knew himself. It would be an invasion of her privacy to give him the third degree. But that didn't mean he might not volunteer something before Rob kicked his ass out of town.

Once he found him, but finding him wasn't going to be a problem.

In Big Falls, there were two kinds of people. Locals and tourists, coming for a meal or a beer at The Long Branch in between visiting the ghost towns nearby. The big guy was neither, and would be as noticeable as the stripe on a skunk's back.

# CHAPTER SIX

*W*hat Kiley needed right then was money. Just a little bit, just enough for gas and so she wouldn't look like a pauper to the Brands and McIntyres if some occasion came that required her to pony-up a few bucks.

Yes, she wanted to go straight. And she was going to! She just needed a little bit, just to keep her afloat until the ranch started making money.

She dug through the car in search of anything she could use to make some scratch. There was a clipboard in her backseat. The prescription bottle was still in her purse, and so were her phony baloney-black rimmed glasses.

Okay, she thought. It's on.

Twenty minutes later, her hair bundled up, glasses in place, clipboard holding an oil change receipt she'd salvaged from the glove compartment, she was knocking at the front door of a massive farm about twenty miles north of Holiday Ranch.

The woman who answered the door was rosy cheeked and friendly, with hair that looked like she was going for ginger dreadlocks, but maybe just looked that way naturally.

"Hi! I'm Ms. K, from Farm-Labs over in Tucker Lake," Kiley said, letting her natural OK twang win the woman's trust.

"Well, hey there. Aren't you a pretty thing? What brings you all the way out here?" Her smile was infectious. It reached her eyes. She was probably forty-something, round and happy. Not one bit unwelcoming.

"We're a brand new lab in Tucker Lake, and we're going around offering a big discount on soil testing to all the farmers in the area."

She lifted her brows. "Well, my husband's the dirt expert, but I can listen to your offer and pass it along. What do you test for? Contaminants or—"

"Well, that would show up, yes, but our main goal—"

"I'm sorry! What am I thinking, letting you stand here on the porch? You wanna come inside? I just made a fresh pot of coffee."

Her brain went, *Huh*? She had to wrestle it back from trying to compute the invitation, so she babbled. "Oh, no, really, um—" She'd been away too long, living in places where people didn't just invite strangers in for coffee. "I'm not s'posed to go inside," she said, coming up with something at last. "Company policy. Besides, this is, um..."

"Now I've gone and thrown you off your game, haven't I hon?" she said. "I'm sorry. Are you nervous?"

Yes, she was nervous as hell, she realized. She was never nervous before a con. Terrible at them, failed at them more often than not, and felt like crap when she succeeded, but she had never been nervous before or during a con. And a tiny little game like this was barely even enough to qualify as one.

"I'm...new. It's my first day, really. And I just really need to do well."

"Aw, isn't that sweet? Okay, go on. I'll shut up and let you give the pitch. Your soil test's goal is to look for..."

"Um, right. Minerals and proteins." Were proteins a soil

thing? "Our test results tell farmers exactly what their soil has in it and what it needs, optimized for your intended crop. In a couple of weeks you get a full report in the mail."

"Isn't it awfully late in the year, though?" she asked.

"We do it now so you can add...um...supplements after the fall harvest. Then you'll have prime ground come spring planting."

"Supplements, huh?"

Kiley got the feeling the woman was starting to see through the act. "Most of our clients double their crop yield when they follow our recommendations."

"Double? Well, I'll be." She took a deep breath, looking Kiley over thoroughly, then looking past her.

Kiley resisted the urge to turn around and see what her car looked like from there. She'd deliberately left it on the side of the road out front, coming up the driveway on foot.

"How much?" the mark finally asked.

"We're doing it for cost, just to show people in the area how good our service is," she said. "It's only fifty bucks. It'll go up next year, but that's the introductory rate."

The farm woman looked at her for a long moment, right into her eyes, in the most uncomfortable way. Then she seemed to come to a decision. "You hold on just a sec, sug." And she walked away from the door, but left it standing open.

Kiley didn't know what to do. She was pretty sure the jig was up, and for all she knew the woman was calling the police right now.

Before she could decide whether to run, though, she was back with two twenties and a ten in one hand, and a plateful of big, steaming, melty chocolate chip cookies in the other. She handed Kiley the cash.

"Oh. Um, thank you," she said, taking it and clipping it to the clipboard, because that seemed more official than stuffing it into her pocket. "And, um, I already have your name and address, so we're all set. You won't regret this."

"No, I'm sure I won't," she said. "And if anything should happen and those test results aren't gonna show up after all, you can leave that fifty right in the mailbox there." She nodded toward the end of the driveway. "You know, whenever you can."

Kiley looked that way, saw the mailbox on a post.

"Now take a cookie for the road. I just baked this batch."

"I shouldn't." Her mouth was dry, her stomach knotted up or something.

"No, you really should. I make the best cookies around. You can ask anyone."

She had the prettiest green eyes, Kiley thought. She hadn't looked at the woman's eyes, she realized, until just then. There was something...beautiful in them.

"Go on, take one. I'm not letting you leave until you do."

Kiley took a cookie. The knot in her stomach pulsed, sending waves out into her chest. It was a new sort of feeling. She pushed it back down to be considered later. "Thank you. Everyone around here is so...nice."

"So are you, honey." No, I'm not, she thought. "Otherwise, you wouldn't be here."

That caught Kiley's attention. "What do you mean?"

She just smiled. "The old folks say this part of Oklahoma chooses her residents. Oh the folks south of us in Big Falls, say it's their town, but the old folks considered this entire part of the state to be...kind of special that way. People meant to be here find their way here, and even if they never intended to stay, somehow, they always do."

Kiley didn't remember ever hearing anything like that. Then again, they'd left Big Falls when she was only twelve.

"You have a beautiful day, now," the farm woman said, and then she closed the door.

Munching on the cookie as she walked back toward the car,

Kiley looked around her at the spread. The white farm house was sprawling and immaculate. Its full front porch had hanging baskets of flowers between every post. There was a gigantic barn that looked new. It stood beside an older one that was now being used to house equipment. Through wide open doors, she could see tractors and other hulking hunks of machinery she couldn't have named if she'd wanted to. The car in the driveway was a big SUV, brand new, American made, top of the line. There was an in-ground pool off one side of the house, just past a sprawling deck.

They had money. This was a very successful operation. Fifty bucks wouldn't even cause a ripple in their financial well-being. For her, it was survival.

Then why did it feel so awful? Why did it *always* feel so awful? And why was this time worse than ever before?

As she drove home, her father's voice whispered through her memory.

*A conscience is a very dangerous thing, girls. It makes you a patsy. Makes you weak. Makes you put the well-being of others ahead of your own, and folks who do that don't make it very far in this world. You just remember that. You start feeling any kind of discomfort inside when you're running a game, that's what it is, that's a conscience trying to take hold of you. And once it gets you, it won't let go and then you're done for. You fight it, you hear?*

Kiley nodded at the voice, dear and beloved and familiar, inside her head. She hadn't visited her father at the Oklahoma State Penn since she'd found out about her sister's death. She'd written him a long letter instead; told him that the ranch was gonna be sold at a tax auction, and that she'd decided to go home to try to get it back. She'd told him she wanted to go straight after that, and that she was sorry she was such a miserable failure at what, for him, was the family business. Jack Marian Kellogg was one of the greats among grifters. It was a source of pride to him.

Turning her back on the life was like a rejection of everything he was. But she poured her heart out in that letter, to try to make him understand.

He hadn't written back.

~

Rob was at Armstrong's garage, located right at the busiest crossroads on Main Street, at the very east edge of the village. He was sitting on a cinder block retaining wall, talking to Edie's husband Wade and watching the vehicles that passed for signs of the stranger. Finding the hulk who'd been asking about Kiley was his real reason for coming into town. He'd been all through the village with no luck, and decided to stop at Wades' to talk about his barn find.

"It's an old El Camino," he said. "Not rusty, either, which is a small miracle."

"Low humidity," Wade said. "Old cars love Oklahoma."

"I don't know if it even runs."

"You find a key for it?" Wade asked. The block wall they were sitting on lined the parking area in front of his shop. It was in the shadow of the building, protecting them from the brilliant, blazing sun.

"They were in the ashtray, believe it or not," Rob said. "Battery's dead though."

Wade nodded. "Is it accessible?"

"I can get it that way with a couple of hours and some elbow grease."

Wade nodded. "I'll bring a tow truck out and haul it back here. Sounds like a fun project."

"You've gotta charge me, Wade," he said. "You know I can afford to pay."

Wade shook his head. "What you can afford doesn't have anything to do with it. Family only pays for parts."

"I get that, but it's not exactly *for* me."

"Ah. For Kiley, then?"

"She's in dire straits. That car she's driving—"

"Yeah, I've seen it. Heard it, too." He gave an expressive shudder. Then he looked right into Rob's eyes and said, "According to Selene, we might as well start calling her family."

"I don't...it isn't... I'm not really...."

"Yeah, I can see you're not. I'll get on it today then." He slid off the stone wall.

"Wait, what do you think Selene meant by that?" He slid off the wall, too.

"Does anyone really know the meaning of *anything* Selene says?" Wade asked. He reached to shake Rob's hand, but when Rob glanced up he saw the guy he'd spent the morning looking for and froze.

The man from Selene's photo was on the other side of Main Street at the gas station, pumping gas into a jacked-up, orange Charger.

Rob took a single step in that direction, and Wade clapped a hand onto his shoulder and said, "That him?"

He nodded. "I need to talk to him."

"I need to come with you."

"No, you really don't, Wade. It's all good."

"You sure?"

"Sure I'm sure."

"He's pretty big," Wade said. "How about I come with you and just watch your back? You know, from a distance?"

Rob glanced over his shoulder at his stepbrother-in-law. "You don't think I'm up to it?"

"I didn't say that." Wade looked at the guy again, grimaced a little. "Do *you* think you're up to it?"

Rob watched the guy pumping gas for a couple more seconds. "Why don't you just watch my back? You know, from a distance."

Wade clapped him on the shoulder and Rob started to walk away, then turned and said, "Don't send out a bulletin just yet, okay?"

Wade, who already had his phone in his hand, slid it back into his pocket. "Sorry. Gets to be a reflex, once you're in the family for a while."

Rob crossed the lazy street to the gas station, walked up to the fellow just as he replaced the gas pump nozzle, and said, "Excuse me."

The guy turned, straightening to his full height as he did. He was 6'6 in his socks. "What?" he asked, and not in a friendly way.

Rob cleared his throat. "I heard you were asking around about a friend of mine."

"You know where she is?"

"Not at the moment, no. What do you want with her?"

The big guy's brows went up. He looked Rob up and down once, then shook his head. "None of your business." Then he turned away, heading around his car toward the driver's side.

Rob waylaid him between the headlights, grabbing his arm and pulling him to a halt. "Not good enough, pal. So I'll ask you again, why are you looking for her?"

He turned slowly. "You really want to do this?"

No, his brain whispered. You really do *not* want this. "What I want is to have a conversation."

"You're about to have a conversation with my fist." The stranger lifted said fist, and Rob thought he was just showing it off, until it hammered his jaw with the approximate force of a wrecking ball.

Rob went down like a sack of feed, rubbed his jaw, which was, incredibly, still attached, and then got up again. "That was uncalled for."

The guy grinned and lifted his fist again.

Rob ducked the blow this time, and drove a good one right

into the thug's middle. The stranger might be big, but Rob was quick, and just as strong. He bobbed beneath another strike, then delivered an uppercut to the chin when he popped up again. After that, he couldn't really keep track of who hit who. The pain in his face and body was about equal to the pain in his fists, so he figured it was a pretty even match. A couple of whoops of encouragement from passersby let him know he was doing okay, and then somehow or other, his two brothers were grabbing him and dragging him a few yards away.

Jason handed him a handkerchief and said, "Nose."

The other dude was still back by his car. Wade had him by one arm, and Caleb, in his suit and tie, had him by the other. Guy was thrashing to get free until Big Falls police chief Jimmy Corona came running from the station a few hundred feet away.

He stopped in front of the stranger, touched his gun and said, "Don't make this harder than it has to be, friend. Just settle down." Then he glanced Rob's way. "You okay?"

"Fine. He's the one who needs a paramedic."

"In your dreams," the stranger said.

"That's enough." Jimmy had been promoted to chief when the old one had retired last year. He was Kara Brand's husband, and he had the leadership gene in him. Peopled respected him. The uniform helped. "Here's what's gonna happen," he told the guy. "You're gonna man up, answer a few questions and more likely than not, get back into this sweet ride of yours, and drive right back where you came from. Are we clear?"

Reluctantly, and maybe a little pacified by the praise of his wheels—it *was* a pretty sweet ride—the stranger said, "Fine."

At Jimmy's nod, Wade and Caleb let go of him.

"I get it," he said with a resentful look at Rob. "You've got friends. That's okay. I've got friends, too."

Wade stepped up to Rob's side, clapped a hand to his shoulder. "We're not friends, pal. We're family."

The fellow sighed and walked toward the Charger's door.

Jimmy stepped in between him and it. "What part of 'you're gonna answer some questions' did you not understand? I need to see some ID."

He stopped moving, but didn't reach for his walled.

"Or I can arrest you for assault," the chief put in.

"You'd have to arrest him, too."

"Him?" Jimmy asked, sending a look Rob's way. "I'm not gonna arrest *him*."

The guy frowned, then said, "Don't tell me you're family, too."

"Stepbrother-in-law or something. It's complicated. ID?"

The guy yanked his license out of his wallet and handed it to Jimmy. Jimmy read the info aloud, probably because he knew Rob wanted it. "Dax J. Russell from Passaic New Jersey." He glanced at another cop who'd finally come across the street to back him up. "Run this for me while I talk to Mr. Russell?"

Nodding, the other cop headed back across Main Street, and up the sidewalk to the Big Falls Police Department.

"You want to tell me what your business is in town, Mr. Russell?"

"It's personal."

"Well, it stops being personal when you assault the police chief's stepbrother-in-law at a local business. Matter of fact, if Rob wants to press charges, I'll have to arrest you right here and now." He glanced Rob's way. "You want to press charges, Rob?"

"All I want is some answers."

"All he wants is some answers," Jimmy said.

"And I'd like them privately," Rob went on.

Jimmy met his eyes, nodded once, turned back to the guy. "I'll tell you what. We're gonna stand over by the pop machine, give you two a minute to yourselves."

The stranger was furious. Rob totally understood why. Small town, everyone related, cops defending the locals. They were playing right into every stereotype this guy probably had before arriving in Big Falls. But it didn't matter, he needed answers and he needed them now.

Not enough to invade Kiley's privacy or unearth whatever secrets she was keeping—though it was damned tempting to try. He only needed to know enough to make sure she was safe. Anything beyond that would be breaking his own rules.

As soon as everyone was out of earshot, he looked the man in the eye—the one that wasn't swollen shut and turning purple —and said, "Why are you looking for Kiley?"

"Is that what she's calling herself now? Kiley?"

"What do you want from her?" Rob asked again.

"She owes me money. If you're involved with her, she'll owe you too, soon enough. She's a crook. A con artist, pal. And you deserve her."

Rob lifted his brows.

"That's all I have to say. Have me arrested if you want to hear more. I'll give your brother the cop all the details, and when I finish, she'll be in a cell right next to me."

Someone pulled up behind the Charger, waiting for the gas pump. Rob got right up in the guy's face. "Get out of town. You hear me? Get out of town. If I find you anywhere near Kiley again, it's not gonna be pretty. Whatever happened between you is over. Done. Cut your losses, and move on, friend."

"Cut my losses?" He sneered, but then winced due to his split lip, ruining the effect as he got into his car and cranked the engine to life. It sounded like thunder. "You deserve her. But just so you know, her name's not Kiley. It's Kendra."

He laid rubber as he left of the station.

~

Kiley had gone through several boxes to decide on the best-looking curtains, and was hanging them when she heard Rob pull in. She had planned to drive to a flea market in Tucker Lake today to look for bargains for the ranch with the fifty bucks she'd made, but for some reason, she'd come home instead.

The living room was really taking shape. The braided rug looked like it belonged there, and the mismatched furniture was in a nicer arrangement. A big truck had pulled in earlier with a delivery that had her just about giddy. A big screen TV and wall-mount kit, with a card that said, "Happy Housewarming, Love Dad." Not her dad, of course. Rob's dad, the billionaire turned small-town saloon owner, RJR McIntyre. Bobby Joe to his friends.

She heard the door close, but remained where she was on the small step ladder, straightening bronze colored sheer panels over the tall windows.

"Wow, this place looks fantastic."

She smiled, hugely pleased. "I've always been good at making a place feel homey," she said. Even when she lived in a closet, she thought. Then she turned to look down at him, gasped in horror and almost fell off the ladder. "Oh my God, what happened? Were you in an accident? Did you wreck your truck?"

"No, and no. It's...a long story." He was standing in the kitchen, looking through the doorway at her.

She hopped off the ladder and got up close, frowning at one part of his face after another and wincing. His lip was split, and he had a bruise forming on one gorgeous cheekbone.

"You have to tell me. But sit down. You can talk while I fix you up." She pushed him backwards into a kitchen chair. "You got into a fight, didn't you?"

"That I did. That I did. And for once, my oversized, meddling family was a good thing to have around."

She spread a dishtowel on the counter, then cracked an ice cube tray onto it, wrapped the ice inside and pressed it to his cheekbone. "Keep it there 'til you can't stand it, and then move it to your poor lip."

He replaced her hand with his. "Thanks."

"So what happened?"

He sighed. "Some big guy from Jersey has been showing a photo of you around town and asking about you."

She frowned for a long moment, processing that, and when she did, it felt like something in the center of her chest melted a little. "You got into a fight because some stranger was asking about *me?*"

He shrugged. "The fight wasn't part of the plan."

"Still, you...you *defended* me?"

"Of course I defended you. You'd do the same for me."

She wasn't so sure she would. Her philosophy was to always do what was best for herself. Getting in front of a set of fists on someone else's behalf didn't seem like the kind of thing she would do at all. But then, unbidden, the image of some big guy pounding on Rob's face came floating into her mind, and her imaginary reaction was to jump on the ape and beat him about the head with her fists.

Wow. That was different.

"Who won the fight?" she asked at length. Because she couldn't think of anything else to say.

"The family intervened before it got very far. But I'm confident I did more damage than he did."

"The daring daughters of Vidalia Brand?" she asked, wide eyed.

"Sounds like an Irish folk group. But no, it was the uh, the scrapping sons-in-law of Vidalia Brand, with back-up by the boisterous brothers of Robert McIntyre."

"I have to hear this. I'm fascinated by this family of yours. I've never known anyone like them."

"Probably never will, either."

She took his hand and led him back to the living room like a lost child, but when his thumb rubbed the back of her hand, it felt intimate and scary.

"I was at Wade's garage. That's the building on Main Street, right across from the gas station."

"Right. Got it. What were you doing there?"

"I was talking to him about that old heap in the barn. It's in a lot better shape than what you're driving, from what I can tell. So he's gonna come get it and see if he can bring it back to life. By the way, we need to move some crap in the morning, early. He's sending a tow truck and we need to make sure he has a clear path to haul the thing out."

She nodded. So not only the fight, but his entire day, had been about her. That was just...weird. "That's awfully nice of you." They were back in the living room, standing in front of the sofa. He was still holding her hand. And she was starting to like it.

"That's what friends are for. So anyway, Selene sent out a group text with this dude's mugshot. She said he'd been in the diner asking about you, and acting all angry and impatient. While I was talking with Wade—"

"Wait, that's what that text was this morning?"

He nodded. "Yeah, they do that."

"Like a Brand-McIntyre All-Points Bulletin."

"Exactly like that," he said. "You catch on fast."

She nudged him toward the sofa. He sank onto it and winced when he leaned back. He had more damage than just what showed on his face. She ran to the kitchen, grabbed more ice in another dishtowel, and brought it back to him. He leaned his head on the sofa's arm, stretching out to his full length. She sat on the edge, laid the ice bundle in her lap, and started to unbutton his shirt. She did the first button quickly, and was almost finished with the second before she realized how silent and still he'd gone. She couldn't bring herself to meet his eyes, but she couldn't stop either. Her hands trembled as she released the third button. She tried to make the fourth one quick, and pushed his shirt open.

And then her gaze kind of got stuck on his abs, because *damn*. And when she tried to focus elsewhere, it stopped on his chest, and her heart started hammering.

His hand covered hers on his chest. She jerked her eyes to his, and saw the fire behind the pain. He was feeling all turned on, too. Oh my God, this was getting complicated.

She tried to remember what she was supposed to be doing, looked at his chest again, focused on the purple bruises forming on his ribcage, and laid the ice there.

He sucked air through his teeth at the cold, and she pulled his shirt closed over the towel, just so she could think straight.

"Are they broken?" she asked in a whisper. Her stomach was all knotted up.

"Nah, just bruised."

"So tell me the story," she said. Because she needed a distraction from thinking about what sex with him would be like. Pretty amazing, she'd bet. "You were talking to Wade, and...?"

"I saw the guy filling up at the gas station and went over to talk to him. That's all I planned to do. Talk to him." He paused. "Probably. Maybe not. Wade wanted to back me up, and I told him to stay out of it."

"And did he?"

"He sent out a family APB, and then he headed over to back me up. By that time, I was in the process of kicking the oversized thug's ass into next Christmas when Jason and Joey appeared out of nowhere to pull me away from him. And Jimmy was standing there with one hand on his gun threatening to make an arrest."

"Jimmy...."

"Kara's husband. He's Chief of Police."

"I'm never even gonna learn all their names, much less their jobs."

"I'll make you some flash cards." He gave her that smile of his that made his eyes crinkle up and sparkle. And then he winced, probably because it hurt to smile.

Kiley closed her eyes. "I'm sorry, Rob. I'm really, *really* sorry if someone I pissed off is in town trying to hunt me down and causing problems for you."

"But not surprised," he said.

She straightened, found him looking at her face. She tried to look right back, but it was hard. His shirt slid open again as he shifted position. Her eyes kept darting to his magnificent, broad, strong, tanned chest.

"Why do you think I'm not surprised?" she asked, only half paying attention to the question or its answer.

"You didn't act surprised. Didn't ask who he was or what he wanted or—"

"Sue me for being more concerned about your cuts and bruises than about the guy who put them there." He was watching her face, looking into her eyes like he could see inside her.

"You need a doctor."

"That would be cousin Sophie. You haven't met her yet. But no, I don't need her for this."

"Well, you at least need some ibuprofen. Be right back." She headed into the bathroom, waited there, trying to get clear on how a normal person acts when they hear a stranger has come looking for them. Surprised, right? But she'd already blown that. Maybe they would also be baffled and unsure why anyone might be looking for them. And maybe they'd be curious or even a little bit scared.

She wouldn't have to fake that part. She'd wronged a lot of people in her life. But she'd kept a list. She never knew why she was doing it, but she had... ever since her first scam, selling Kevin Henderson a joint made out of rolling paper and pencil shavings in the sixth grade. But she'd written down the name and address of every person she'd ever conned, with the dollar amount beside it.

It occurred to her that maybe she was supposed to pay them all back. But that was a stupid idea. It would be next to impossible for her to do. She didn't even have a job. And what good would it do, anyway? Most of them probably didn't even remember. Some of them didn't even know they'd been scammed.

And yet, the thought occurred to her again. It kept doing that every couple of weeks or so.

It felt as if there was a cocoon in her core, one she'd always sort of sensed there, but now it was breaking open. Something was alive inside it, some new part of her was emerging. It was scary as hell.

Okay, okay, this all bore thought, but later. She shook loose a couple of ibuprofen from the bottle in the medicine cabinet, took them back downstairs and handed them to Rob, who was hobbling back from the kitchen with an open long neck in one hand.

"Rob, you should've let me get that."

"It's purely for the pain," he said, sinking back into his spot on the sofa, moving slow, grimacing a little.

When he lay down, she put the two tablets into his hand and said. "So is this."

He swallowed the pills with a drink of beer. "Thank you, Kiley."

"I think you were the one who said doing nice things for each other would be good for our business relationship. I'm just following your suggestion. So on that note, why don't you relax here and let me make our dinner tonight."

He nodded, but when she turned to go, he caught hold of her hand and pulled until she sat down beside him again. "Do you know any oversized thug who would have reason to come looking for you?"

"Of course not."

He touched her face, turned it so he could look her right in the eyes. "I promise I won't judge you, no matter what you ever tell me about yourself. You get that, right?"

"Yeah. I get that." It was hard to believe, but she was starting to think it was the truth.

"And you don't have to tell me anything you don't want to. But I've gotta ask you for a promise in return. I'd really be grateful, Kiley, if you could promise not to lie to me. I'd rather have you tell me nothing at all, than tell me a lie."

His eyes were so intense that she knew this was a big, fat deal to him. And she'd like to know why. Hell, he was so big on honesty that maybe if she asked him, he'd tell her.

She took a deep breath, then sighed and figured what the hell. He'd fought for her today. She probably owed him something. "Okay. I promise that I'll...try my best not to lie to you. And the answer to your other question is, yeah, I can think of several thugs who might have an ax to grind with me."

He lifted his brows and she thought his surprise was real.

"Sometimes...in the past...I've...maybe...used men, a little bit, to get...you know, what I wanted." Then she shrugged. "But I mean, they used me to get what they wanted, too, so it's really pretty much even. Though they... probably wouldn't see it that way."

He nodded. "This guy, he called you a criminal and a con artist."

That hurt. She frowned hard in reaction to it and said, "I am *not* a criminal."

Rob seemed to consider that for a long moment. "He said you owed him money."

"That really doesn't narrow it down much," she admitted. "Did he give you a name?"

"Dax J. Russell." Rob pulled out his phone and scrolled to the photo Selene had sent. "From New Jersey."

"I've never even *been* to Jersey." He turned the phone to show her the guy's face. She looked at it, then frowned and looked closer. "My God, he's *huge*."

"Huger in person."

Lowering the phone, she looked into Rob's eyes and said, "I don't know this man, Robby. That's the truth. I've pissed off a lot of men in my past, but this guy is not one of them." She handed the phone back to him.

He was looking at her hard, looking for signs she was lying. And that hurt a little, though it shouldn't. She closed her eyes, lowered her head. Part of her wanted to tell him that she'd been both of those things, a criminal and con artist, for her entire life. Right up until she'd decided to change.

And it was only just then that she realized something inside her *was* changing. Up until that moment, it had only been words. A vague intention. *I'm going to change.* Now it felt more like, *I'm changing.*

"He said your name wasn't even Kiley. Just as he left, he said that."

She blew air between her teeth. "Well now I *know* he's a liar. What is it, then?"

"Kendra," he said. "Wasn't that your sister's name?"

She blinked. Just hearing her sister's name brought the pain rushing back to her. "Yeah."

"Where was she when she died, Kiley?"

*Don't tell him. Don't tell him. Don't tell him.*

"New Jersey."

*Why did I tell him?*

"Do you...I mean, did you look that much alike? That Selene and Edie could see a photo of her and think it was you?" he asked.

She met his eyes, and knew she was in too far to back off now.

"Probably," she said. "Her eyes are green, mine are blue." She got up and walked to the kitchen. "You have any ideas about dinner?" she asked, and her voice came out deep and thick. "I'm not a great cook, I'll warn you in advance." Dammit, there were hot tears burning down her cheeks. She kept her back to him, started opening cupboards and the fridge as if looking for ideas. But she wasn't seeing anything but her sister's face.

# CHAPTER SEVEN

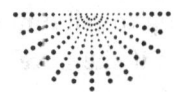

*H*earing Kendra's name had hit Kiley like a mallet. Rob had seen it very clearly. She'd tried hard to hide her reaction, but he'd seen it. Shock had paled her skin and widened her eyes and caused her full lips to part on a soft gasp. There had been tears welling before she'd managed to shoot off the sofa and head for the kitchen. Real tears.

Kiley hadn't denied she was a con artist. She'd implied there could be a number of men angry and claiming she owed them money.

She seemed to feel genuinely bad that he'd gotten into a violent altercation on her behalf, though. And she was trying, she really was, to give him a few crumbs of honesty.

Maybe it was enough for one night. That guy, whatever else he might be, was big and damn scary to a little thing like Kiley. Rob would defend her against him whether she was in the right or in the wrong.

The problem was, he liked her. He liked her a lot. He even liked her shady ways. And he was attracted to her, too, in a purely physical, me-Tarzan-you-Jane sort of way. He hadn't felt like that in a long, long time.

But the lies. God, he felt them hanging over his head like Poe's pendulum, swinging closer with every pass. The only difference was, *he* wasn't strapped down. He was voluntarily lying there, waiting for it to gut him.

Or for her to come clean, and pull the lever that would stop its deadly swinging. She was the only one who could. His goal in life, right then, crystallized for him. He was going to win Kiley's trust. She was going to tell him everything about herself of her own free will. Even if she never showed anyone else her true self, she would show him.

She puttered around in the kitchen, finally putting some homemade chicken pot pies, courtesy of Vidalia, into the oven and setting the timer. While they cooked, she did other things. Noisy things. She might have been washing dishes. He was too busy trying to figure out whether Dax Russell actually knew her or not.

Eventually, he gave up, and looked around the room. Something was different. And then he realized what. A very large television was mounted to the wall in front of him. How he'd missed it, he didn't know.

Yes he did. When Kiley was around, he didn't notice much else.

"Hey, was the TV fairy here?"

She leaned through the doorway from the kitchen. "Isn't it amazing? The remote's on the coffee table."

He reached for it and hit the power button.

"How did you manage to mount it by yourself?"

She didn't come in, just called from the kitchen. "I'm not all *that* handy. I called the cable company, but there's no cable on our road. So then I called the satellite dish people. They said they couldn't come for a week, but I asked them to come today instead."

"And they just agreed?"

"Well, yeah." She hesitated. "I kind of...talked them into it."

"Uh-huh. And how did you do that, exactly?" He listened intently, but all the same, started skimming channels.

When she spoke again her voice was closer, and he turned. She was leaning in the doorway again, a potholder in her hand, looking at the big screen. "I *might've* said that my husband was going to be one of the guest pundits on *Meet the Press* this week. He's a journalist and it's his first appearance, and I promised not to miss it and...."

"And they came right out," he said.

She nodded. "It was only a little white lie."

"And the fellow who showed up to turn things on just...decided to do the wall mount to be a nice guy?"

She shrugged. "You may not have noticed, Rob, but I clean up kind of nice, and I can flirt pretty well. I didn't lie at all. Not even a little bit. He just volunteered."

He looked her over and realized that, yes, she was wearing makeup, and she'd done something sexy to her hair, flipping it all over to one side and letting those waves cascade down to her shoulders. She wore a snug-fitting tank top with a soft cotton shirt over it, unbuttoned, and jeans that fit her like a second skin.

"Don't judge. You promised that if I was honest, you wouldn't judge."

"I'm not judging." He shrugged, let his eyes roam down to her feet and up again, and said, "Well, I am, but only to the point of thinking how good you look tonight, and wondering how the hell it took me this long to notice."

"Cause I've been up in your face and you have one eye swollen shut," she said. "And thanks."

Her cheeks went all soft pink and pretty. Then a timer pinged, and she said, "Find us something amazing to watch while we eat in front of the TV like a couple of uncivilized savages. I'll bring dinner right in."

So he channel surfed, found a comedy that had something

for both of them. She brought in the pot pies on giant plates, spread out to cool more quickly, and set them on the coffee table.

"It smells fantastic."

"Yeah, I'm a wiz at reading instructions and setting oven timers," she said.

"I smell something else." He looked toward the kitchen, following the scent. "Chocolate?"

"I threw a brownie mix in while the pies were baking. They should be just cooled off enough by the time we're ready for dessert." She sat down beside him. "Are you mad at me?" she asked. "For lying to the TV people?"

He looked at her freckles, thought about how much he liked her, in spite of the secrets she was keeping. And he said, "It's none of my business who you lie to. I'm trying hard to win your trust, here, Kiley, in case you haven't noticed that. The only time I'm gonna care about lies is if you lie to me. Okay?"

She seemed to think about that for a long moment. To really let it sink in. And then she said, "There are things...I haven't told you. Do you consider that lying?"

He shook his head slowly. "As long as it's not pertinent to us...to our...partnership, our friendship, our business, then you don't have to tell me anything you don't want to." He shrugged. "I'm hoping eventually, you'll want to."

"I'm already starting to want to," she said. "And if you knew how unusual that was for me, you'd be super flattered." She looked down at her plate, moved the veggies and gravy around with her fork, and watched the steam spiral up off them. "I was telling the truth about that Dax guy, though. I don't know who he is. He doesn't look familiar to me at all. And I've never been to Jersey."

Rob nodded. "Okay."

"Okay? You got the stuffing kicked outta you, and you can just say okay, like everything's fine?"

"Everything is fine. And you don't have to worry about that guy, or any other guy like him. Not as long as you're with me."

She just sat there blinking, looking kind of shell shocked and stunned.

~

Caleb Montgomery's law office was on the ground floor of a tall, old-fashioned building that looked as if it could've been standing back when horses instead of cars parked out front. He was married to Maya, the oldest of Vidalia Brand's daughters, Kiley thought as she waited in the leather chair in his reception area, wondering why there was no one at the desk.

She knew Caleb was in his office, but the door was closed and she could hear voices from the other side, so she wasn't going to knock and interrupt. She'd just wait.

Damned if she'd ever thought she'd be sitting in a lawyer's office, short of needing one to defend her. But here she was. Life sure did change.

The big wooden door opened, and a very tall, beautiful blond woman came out, dabbing her eyes with a tissue. She spotted Kiley sitting there, and quickly sniffled and tucked the tissue out of sight. "So sorry to keep you waiting," she said. "I didn't think we had any appointments until—"

"I don't have an appointment," Kiley said. "I was hoping Mr. Montgomery could sort of squeeze me in."

She glanced past the woman, who turned out to be the missing receptionist, through the still-open door into the office.

The lawyer was already smiling at her from the doorway. "Kiley. Brenda, this is Rob McIntyre's new partner. Kiley, my receptionist, Brenda."

"Hello," Kiley said to the blonde. She was seriously curious about why the woman was crying in her boss's office. Seemed suspicious as hell. None of her business, though. Odd how much it pissed her off on Maya's behalf, though. If he was having a fling, he ought to be skinned. She hoped that wasn't it.

"Nice to meet you, Kiley," Brenda said, sliding into her seat at the desk.

"Come on in and tell me what I can do for you," Caleb called. "Brenda, give us a few minutes, okay?"

"Sure, boss."

He waited for Kiley to enter, then closed the office door. Impressive, but not braggy. Bookcases full of books and sturdy leather furniture and a gigantic shiny hardwood desk that looked like an antique. "Nice," she said with a nod. "Thanks for seeing me, Mr. Montgomery."

"Call me Cal. You're practically family." He nodded toward a big chair and when she sank into it, she felt a little like Goldilocks. The thing was huge. "What can I help you with?"

"It's a small favor, really. Nothing big. Shouldn't take you more than a phone call. But um, the thing is, I'd like you to keep it between us."

He nodded. "You got a dollar on you?"

She frowned. "Sure I do."

"Fork it over."

Weird, but okay. She dug in her purse, pulled out the 50 bucks she'd conned out of that farm wife the day before, looked at it for a second, stuffed it back in and kept digging. Eventually, she'd scared up three quarters, two nickels, a dime and five pennies. He held out his hand and she dropped the change in.

"That's my retainer," he said. Not a word about her scraping the bottom of the barrel to get it for him. "You're now my client, and attorney-client privilege applies."

She sighed in relief, leaned back in the giant chair, and thought he didn't seem like the kind of guy who'd cheat. "So, I'm sure you know about the guy who was asking about me around town yesterday?" He nodded. "I want to track him down and find out what he wants."

"Oh." He grimaced and sucked air through his teeth. "I...don't know about that."

"Why?"

"Just...he seemed angry and...dangerous. And big."

"I could see that from the picture." And from the condition of Rob's gorgeous face.

"But you don't know him," he said.

She shook her head. "No. But I want to know what's up. I guess...Rob said your brother-in-law the cop took his info. I just want his number. I want to see this photo he's been showing around town of me and find out what he's up to."

"Guess I can't blame you for that." He picked up a pencil and rolled it between his thumb and forefinger for a minute. "What if I could track him down and talk to him on your behalf."

She shook her head. "No. I need to talk to him myself."

He nodded, tapping the pencil on the edge of his desk. There were little marks that suggested he did that a lot. "Would you object to me going with you? Maybe standing in the shadows, out of earshot? It would give you privacy for your discussion, and protection in case he has anything...unpleasant on his mind."

"Not necessary. I'm not scared of him." She'd been dealing with men, crooks as well as marks, her whole life. She'd never met one she couldn't either outsmart or flirt into submission. "I really need to do this myself. Can you get me the information?"

He nodded. "I can. I will. I'll call the PD and ask for it. However, you should be aware there's a good chance Jimmy—Chief Corona—is gonna ask why I want it. And I'm gonna have to tell him it's for a client and therefore privileged, and he's gonna figure it's either you or Rob."

She sighed. "Well that kind of stinks for my privacy."

He nodded. "It does. If you're sticking around Big Falls, and I assume you are, being that you just bought a ranch, I should warn you that there's not much that goes unnoticed. Small town. Huge grapevine. And the family...." He just shook his head.

"Yeah, I got that already." She smiled involuntarily. "It's kind of nice, actually."

"And kind of not," he said. "But the nice outweighs the not, and you get used to it. You even start to rely on it. I'll be as sly as I can, okay?"

"Okay."

He picked up his phone, punched a button. "Hey, Brenda. Get me Lucy at the BFPD front desk, will you?"

He waited a second, drumming his fingers, then sat up straighter. "Hi, Lucy. It's Cal at the law office. Fine, and yours?" Smiling, laughing. Was everyone in this town friends with everyone else? "Listen, Lucy, I need the info on that guy who got into the fight at Gregg's Gas & Go yesterday." There was a pause, and then he was scribbling on a notepad. "No, not for vengeance," he said with a laugh. "This is strictly business. Thanks, Lucy." He hung up the phone, tore the sheet off his notepad and handed it across the desk to her.

Kiley turned it over and looked at it. Dax J. Russell's address, cell phone, and home phone numbers, along with his birthdate, driver's license ID number, and the make, model and plate number of his car were written in easy-to-read block letters. "Wow. That was easy."

"It was, and Lucy didn't ask who it was for, just whether I was out to avenge Rob's black eye." He smiled. He was genuinely nice, she thought. This town was apparently full of unicorns. "Now I have a question for you."

"Shoot," she said.

"You want a job?"

Her brows shot up high. It was the last thing she'd expected him to say. "What, here?"

"Yeah. My secretary just gave notice. She's moving to Memphis. Her husband got a job offer he couldn't turn down.

You probably noticed the tears. She's been here a long time, and she's feeling guilty as hell about leaving me in the lurch."

"But I don't...know anything about...law." Other than how to break it, that was.

"You can answer phones and emails, yes?"

"Well, yeah. Anybody can do that."

"You'd be surprised. Look, my business is small. Local cases, nothing complicated. The main qualification is trustworthiness. Nothing that happens in this office, not even who comes and goes, is to be discussed with anyone besides me. Ever. Can you handle that?"

"Sure can." She sighed. "But I mean, there's going to be so much to do at the ranch."

"There will be. But there's not yet. It's the middle of summer. Too late to plant pumpkins or corn for the corn maze."

"You know about my plans?"

"Rob told me. He thinks you're brilliant, and so do I, by the way."

"He does?" Why did she suddenly feel warm all over?

He smiled wide. "He does. Look, take two weeks to think about it. I'll look for other options in the meantime. No pressure. Okay?"

"Sure. Okay."

All the way back to the ranch, she kept replaying Caleb's words in her head. She had to be trustworthy. That seemed to be a running theme in this family. Truthfulness. Honesty.

Going straight had been kind of an abstract notion to her. In her mind it had meant making enough money in legal ways to allow her to quit having to make it in illegal ways.

But now it was starting to become really clear to her that she'd had it wrong. It wasn't about money at all; it was about people. About being honest and truthful with people. Which meant trusting them enough to make herself vulnerable to them. It was about being the kind of person others could think

97

of as trustworthy too, the kind they felt they could make themselves vulnerable to.

Her father's voice whispered through her memory. *Being honest with other people is like showing your belly and trusting them not to slice it open. Never tell the truth when a lie will do.*

But that was what real honesty seemed to require. Exposing your belly and trusting.

And maybe that had to come before the rest of it. She had to trust people enough. And too, she was starting to think she had to quit the old life completely before the new one could open up for her.

She turned onto Pine Road, but when she got to Holiday Ranch she drove right past, and kept going another half hour north, to that thriving farm where she'd been the day before. She pulled the car off onto the shoulder, took the fifty bucks from her purse, and tucked it into the mailbox.

And then she drove away, feeling as if the weight of the world had lifted from her shoulders. She felt light. Almost giggly, she felt so light. It was some kind of high.

It occurred to her that she would probably get that same feeling again and again if she paid back every person she'd ever conned. And all of the sudden, it didn't seem like such an impossible idea, or a stupid one.

Was that it then? Was she finally going straight? Had she actually gone straight already, instead of just intending to? She thought so. If felt like a defining moment in her life. It felt so important that she had to pull over to the side of the road, because there were tears in her eyes and she couldn't see.

She sat there, mulling, and nodding, and realizing that she had never felt this good about herself in her life. That made her so confident, she decided to face her next challenge head on. She took the note Caleb had given her out of her jean's pocket, and tapped the stranger's number into her cell phone.

# CHAPTER EIGHT

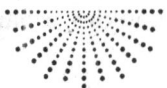

*K*iley figured if she was a normal person, she'd be nervous, heading out to meet with a stranger who was reportedly pretty upset with her sister. She should probably be afraid he wouldn't believe she was Kendra's twin, or that he'd hurt her or something like that.

She wasn't afraid, though. She was more nervous around Rob and his family than she would be around some lowlife thug. And he had to be a lowlife thug, if he'd ever been involved with Kendra. She knew his kind. She knew a hundred. She'd grown up around his kind.

She *was* his kind.

"Not anymore," she whispered.

She parked at a meter, and dutifully put in a quarter instead of just taking her chances like she normally would. "Let 'em ticket me. Good luck getting paid." That's what she'd have muttered at the parking meter once. Respectable people put the darn quarters in.

She was trying to become a better woman, an honest woman —a confident, capable, respected and respectable woman, like those Brand women were.

Any nerves she might've been developing when she reached her destination evaporated as soon as she walked into Maude's. The coffee house was as warm and welcoming as any place she'd ever been, with little sitting areas situated all around, every one of them unique.

It was the kind of place where conversations broke out between strangers on sugar-highs from the mouthwatering treats behind the glass; cookies, eclairs, doughnuts, danishes, even a couple of pies.

"Welcome to Maude's," said a beautiful blonde. "I'm Carly, the owner. And you're a first timer! You get a free treat."

Kiley looked at the glass case and her mouth watered. "Can I get it on the way out? I'm meeting someone. A big grouchy mean guy who's been harassing my sister, and really doesn't deserve a free treat anywhere near as much as my partner Rob does."

The woman pulled in her chin and lifted her brows. "You need backup?"

"Nah, I got this."

"I'll keep an eye on you just in case. Go on, pick a spot. I'll bring you something to drink. Coffee?"

Kiley looked around at the frothy, foamy, pricey drinks others were slurping. Not yet, she thought. But one day soon, it wouldn't be a luxury to order a fancy-assed coffee. "Just a plain coffee, thanks."

"Iced mocha latte is today's special. Same price as a regular coffee. You should try it." Carly's smile was friendly and infectious.

"Okay, I will, thanks." As the woman went to make her latte, Kiley headed to the cozy nook near the fireplace, even though it wasn't burning at the moment. After all, it was July in Oklahoma—no way a fire was going to bring in the customers. More likely to drive them out.

She sat down on a curving leather sofa in front of a glass

table and looked around the place. Everyone who caught her eye flashed a warm smile. A little girl waved at her. She'd forgotten how friendly and intimate small-town life could be. Even here in Tucker Lake, which was a much bigger small-town than Big Falls. She remembered her father complaining about everybody knowing everybody's business, and she'd come back fully prepared to hate that aspect, too.

But it didn't feel at all hateful to her. It felt kind of good. Kind of comforting, and maybe even a little bit secure.

The door jangled, and Kiley looked up to see a man she recognized, but only from the photo on Rob's phone. He was even bigger in person, and when he looked her way and scowled, she was happy to see that he was sporting a black eye, bruised chin, and a cut eyebrow.

*Go, Robby.*

Carly brought a giant mugful of sugar topped in whipped cream trying to pass itself off as coffee, and set it in front of her. Leaning in, she whispered, "That him?"

"Yep."

"I think you need backup."

"Nope."

"I'm calling my dad anyway." She nodded and walked away as Dax J whatever—who looked like what would happen if John Cena and the The Rock made a test-tube baby—strode toward Kiley

She stood up, not to be polite but because the way he was moving toward her was so aggressive she thought he might try to hit her. She could dodge big meaty fists better standing up. He kept coming, looking angrier and angrier.

Reflexively, she held up both hands. "I'm not Kendra."

"The hell you aren't." But he stopped in his tracks, standing right there beside the table near the teardrop-shaped seat across from hers.

"I'm her twin sister, Kiley."

He narrowed his eyes, then his brow impersonated an accordion. "You have blue eyes."

She nodded. "Kendra's are green."

He lifted his brows. "Tinted contacts."

She spread her right eyelid wide and leaned up at him. "You can touch it if you wash your hands first. But I think you can see there's no lens in my eye."

He leaned in. His breath smelled of root beer. He wasn't so scary.

"I'm right handed, she's left. My eyes are blue, hers are green, and besides all of that, there's this." She slapped her proof on the wooden table, a newspaper clipping. She'd made copies in case she ever lost it, but she figured the original would be more impressive in this case.

*Woman, 23, Dies in Tragic Fire.*

He frowned hard at the story. There was a photo of Kendra, and a block of text beside it. Kiley knew what it said by heart. *Kendra Kellogg, who would have been twenty-four years old in September, was killed in a fire that destroyed the house she shared with five other young adults. She is survived by her twin sister, Kiley. The cause of the fire is under investigation.*

The reporter had a heart. Didn't mention the house was a halfway house, or that the five other young adults were five other petty thieves.

She watched him read it. He was a slow reader. Why was she not surprised? Finally he looked up from the clipping and dropped like a boulder into the chair beside her.

Sighing, she said, "Hi, I'm Kiley."

There were tears pooling in his eyes. "I'm Dax," he said. "I can't believe she's really—" He couldn't say it.

Kiley tried to distract herself from a groundswell of emotion by taking a giant sip of the icy, chocolatey coffee flavored drink. She gave herself a cold-headache, closed one eye and rubbed her temple.

Emotion avoided.

"So why are you running around Big Falls flashing a photo of my sister?" She asked. "What did she do to you?"

He opened his mouth, closed it again, shook his head.

Kiley realized he felt ashamed, stupid, because her sister had played him so thoroughly. It was just like Rob said he'd felt over a woman. Kiley was seeing it firsthand, for the first time. "It's what she does, Dax. She's really good at it. One of the best."

"Best at what?"

"At the con. The grift. The game. She took a bunch of money from you, didn't she?"

"No," he said. "I gave it to her."

"Honey, they all give it to her. What did she do? Say she needed surgery?"

His eyes snapped to hers. "A kidney transplant."

"The Slice & Dice with a Side of Beans."

"The what now?"

"Slice & Dice," she made a cutting motion with a butter knife from the table. "As in surgery. Side of beans, as in kidney." He blinked at her. "Kidney? Beans? Kidney beans?"

He shook his head. "You're not pretending. You're nothing like her. Last week when I saw her, she said—"

"Wait, what?"

"When I saw her—"

"Last week?" Kiley interrupted. "Did you say last week?"

"Yeah, last week. When I gave her the money and took her to the airport."

The sound of her own heartbeat thrummed in Kiley's ears. "That's not possible, Dax. Look at the date on that newspaper clipping."

He leaned over the table, then sat up again. "But I've seen her since then. Look, look at the date on this." He took out his cell phone, tapped, scrolled and handed it to her.

Kiley looked at the photo. Her beautiful sister smiled back at her. She was wearing her hair dead straight, and her freckles were covered with enough makeup to choke a bear. Looked like a mortician had done her face, which was fitting, since she was supposed to be dead. "When...when was this taken?"

"At the airport. Newark."

"And where was she heading?"

"That's the thing," Dax said, leaning back in his chair. "She said she had to go to Chicago for her transplant. But she didn't go to that gate. I thought I saw her boarding a flight to Oklahoma City. I remembered her mentioning her hometown of Big Falls, once. That's why I came here."

She tapped the *photos* icon on his phone and scrolled. He had plenty of other shots of her Kendra. And the dates went well past the date of her death.

And suddenly, she got it. It was a con. Kendra's death was nothing but one more great big con.

"That bitch," she whispered. But she had to force herself not to smile. Her sister was alive!

She was going to kill her.

Belatedly remembering the man across from her, she said, "Tell me about you and Kendra. Start at the beginning."

He looked momentarily blissful. "She waited tables at the café where I had lunch every day. I um, work for my father's company."

"Doing what?" she asked.

He looked surprised that she was interested. She was frankly kind of surprised herself. "My father owns lots of businesses. I worked for one of the racetracks."

"Like NASCAR?"

"Horse racing. I manage his track in Saratoga Springs."

She smiled. "You like it?"

"Love the horses. Hate the business. But I get to spend time with trainers and breeders and the horses themselves." He said it all in a rush, maybe before he'd thought it through. Then he said, "I have to spend a couple months a year in Jersey at corporate. Kendra waited on me every day at lunch. I don't know, we flirted a little I guess, and pretty soon I asked her out and we started…you know…being together. A couple. She told me she was gonna die without a kidney transplant…."

"And you gave her money."

"I gave her a lot of money." He sighed. "And then she got a call. Said it was a miracle. They found a match. She had to fly to Chicago right then, have a transplant. I drove her to the airport. And then…."

Kiley gave him a second to breathe. She said, "How do you know she didn't go to the right gate? They wouldn't have let you in without—"

"I bought a ticket."

"Oh, hell." She closed her eyes, her heart breaking for the guy.

"I couldn't let her go through the surgery alone. I left her at the security checkpoint, walked back to the concourse, and bought a ticket for the same flight. But when I got to the gate, she wasn't there. I waited till they boarded the plane. She didn't get on. I stood there like an idiot with a ticket in my hand, and the flight attendant trying to get me to board."

"You had it pretty bad for her, huh?" He sighed, nodded. "As I was walking back up the concourse, I saw her out of the corner of my eye, just stepping out of sight as another flight boarded. I couldn't get in without causing a scene, and you'd have to be suicidal to cause a scene at an airport these days."

"Yeah," she said. "I hear you."

"It was a flight to Oklahoma City. And that's when I realized there was no kidney. She'd conned me. I knew it right then. And I've been looking for her ever since."

The story made perfect sense. Her sister was alive.

But she'd faked her death. She'd done that on purpose, and while Kiley wanted to kick her ass for putting her through what she had, she also wondered if maybe Kendra had a good reason for such drastic measures. What if she was looking at prison time, or if she'd conned the wrong mark? Maybe someone dangerous who was out for revenge?

Her first priority was to protect her sister.

She lifted her head and looked Dax Russell in the eye. "I don't know who scammed you. But this—" she set the leather pouch on the table between them. "—is all that's left of my sister. I've been carrying her ashes around with me for the past month and a half, waiting to spread them where she'd want them."

He didn't believe her. "What are you doing, Kiley? Look at her," he said, flashing the phone in her face. "She's your twin."

"*Kendra* was my twin. That chick on your phone isn't Kendra. If you were female, you'd realize that hair and makeup can pretty much make you look like anybody you want. A con like the one who got you—she'd know that. She probably knew Kendra from back in the day, and knew she'd died, so her name was safe to use."

"Are you conning me, too, now? Is that what this is?"

"I know you don't want to believe it, Dax, but Kendra's dead. Hell, if your chick was the real Kendra, she'd have called herself Shirley or something." She pushed his phone away from her face. "That isn't my sister. And I'm really sorry about the money."

"I borrowed it from my father's company," he said.

"I'm really sorry, Dax."

"I didn't ask first."

"Oh, hell," she whispered.

"Kendra—or whoever she was—said the insurance would pay out within a week or two and she'd reimburse me. I figured I'd put it back and no one would ever know. She said if they waited for all the bullshit red tape, she'd be dead."

Kiley lowered her head.

"I believed her," he said. "I loved her."

"I'm really sorry, Dax." She reached across the table, put a hand on his big forearm. "If it helps, try to realize that you fell in love with the person you thought she was. She's smart enough to figure out what your ideal woman would be, all those lunches she served you, all the small talk you shared. She figured out exactly what you wanted, and then morphed into it, knowing she'd found herself a golden goose. She wasn't really who you thought she was."

"She pretended really well."

"That person, the one she was pretending to be—maybe there's a real version of her out there somewhere. And someday, you're gonna find her."

She got up, picked up her drink, and said, "Thanks for being so...honest. I'm real sorry for your losses, Dax."

He nodded. "Guess this is one of those life lesson deals, right?"

"I guess so." She waved, he nodded, and Kiley went to the register.

He called after her, "It's on me, Kiley."

"And me," the owner said, handing her a bag. "I put a couple of my favorites in there. And if it's okay with you, I'm gonna give Sad-Sack over there his freebie, too."

"Yeah," Kiley said. "Turns out he's a really sweet guy." And she'd just lied to him, and probably broken his heart.

She'd find him and tell him the truth someday, when she knew it would be safe for Kendra.

Kendra.

Her heart swelled up in her chest. God, it was wonderful! Kendra was alive.

# CHAPTER NINE

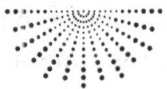

*R*ob finished putting in the stained glass window, glanced at his watch and got a little more worried about Kiley. And then he spotted her headlights. For just a split second, they ignited the stained glass and painted the attic in jewels, ruby and emerald and sapphire.

He was unreasonably glad she was home. That was probably a warning sign. He needed to rein it in before he did something stupid, like falling for her. Smiling, he picked up his tools and heard the front door open. He hurried downstairs to greet her, and was surprised by how dark it was. All the lights were still off. He'd spent more time in the attic than he'd realized. He wondered if Kiley would tell him what she'd been up to today. Probably not.

She walked into the living room, looked at him and froze, like she was surprised to see him there. And then she shifted instantly, ran to him, and said, "Oh thank God, thank God, I've finally found someone who can help me."

She pressed her hands to his chest and said, "I need a man. A big, strong man like you. I need a hero. I need—"

"You need to get your hands off him, Kendra, and you need to do it *now*."

Kiley's voice came from the kitchen door, and then she hit the light switch, and Rob stood there blinking at her. There were tears in her eyes, anger in her frown, and a smile trying to tug her lips upward.

Then he looked at the woman front of him, so similar to Kiley, and yet so different. And he couldn't even pinpoint how. She seemed older. There was a meanness to her. And her eyes were brilliant emerald green.

*Kendra* smiled a big innocent smile. It startled him so much he took a step backward. "You're not Kiley," he said. He couldn't stop looking back and forth between them.

"No, but I bet you'd like me better," Kendra said, and then she turned, looked at her sister. "Hi, Kiley."

Kiley glared, then melted into tears, ran across the room and wrapped her sister in her arms, sobbing, "You're alive, oh my God you're really alive, ohmygod you're *alive*."

Kendra hugged back. They stood there, wrapped around each other like a pair of spider monkeys. Kiley lifted her head from her sister's shoulder and looked his way. Her eyes were very wet and she was kind of smiling in a wobbly way.

He smiled back, getting it. This was the sister she'd thought was dead. He was witnessing a miracle, and he knew he ought to go outside or upstairs or something and let them have some privacy, and he was trying to, he really was. But his feet seemed to have melded with the floor.

And then it was like a switch flipped. Kiley's face went stormy, she pushed Kendra back and slapped her right across the face.

Her head snapped, but she stood steady, taking it like a champ.

"You let me think you were dead!" Kiley shouted. "How

could you do that to me? You let me think you were *dead*, Kendra. That you burned in a freaking *fire*."

Kendra rubbed her cheek. "Yeah, about that—"

"They sent me your *ashes*." Kiley yanked a leather pouch from her purse and threw it. It hit Kendra in the chest, releasing a little puff of dead person dust on impact, before plopping unceremoniously to the floor between them. "Who the hell have I been carrying around with me? Who have I been talking to and crying over?"

Kendra was staring at the pouch at her feet. "Some homeless chick one of the other residents was banging. When I read about my own demise, I figured it was a chance…" She glanced over her shoulder at him. He really had to leave, he thought. "A chance at a fresh start. And I took it." She turned her back to Kiley, making a circle, looking around the living room. "I like what you've done with the place. Cute curtains. Nice TV, too. You have cable?"

Rob was stunned, even though he knew he shouldn't be listening to any of this. Holy shit, she'd *deliberately* let the world think she was dead?

"You had to know they'd notify me," Kiley said.

"You and Dad, yeah." She was inspecting the kitchen now, hands in the pockets of a brown leather jacket that was completely unnecessary tonight.

"Dad thinks you're dead, too?" Kiley asked.

She didn't answer.

"You faked your own death?" The words came out before Rob could stop them. He lowered his head. "Sorry, sorry, I'm going."

Kiley glanced his way briefly, and there was something pleading in her eyes. He held up a hand, nodded, and went into the kitchen, letting the two of them have the living room to themselves.

"I can't believe you did this, Kendra."

"Better than the alternative," she replied.

"You could've found me, told me."

"That's what I'm doing. Or didn't you notice?" She looked around again. "How the hell did you manage to scam the money to buy back the place?"

"Shut up, Kendra."

Kendra shot Rob a look in the kitchen, then nodded once, like she got the message. He was still too close, he thought. He ought to go outside. He reached into the fridge for a beer to take with him, and knew it was true. Kiley had tried to scam him out of half the money to pay for the place. Not for the first time, he wondered how she'd managed to raise the other half.

"Look," Kendra said, lowering her voice a whole lot. "I'm not gonna mess up whatever you've got going here. I just...I need a place to crash. Just for a few days."

"No."

Just like that. But she was *family*. Rob clamped his jaw. This was none of his business. Why the hell hadn't he gone outside yet? He closed the fridge, opened his beer, and headed for the door.

Kendra lowered her head, blinked fast, like she was holding back tears. "Well, where the *hell* am I gonna go, then?"

The door was open and Rob was halfway out. But he stopped where he was and cleared his throat. Two eerily similar gazes, one green, the other as blue as a summer sky, snapped his way. "Um...there might be an empty room at The Long Branch," he said.

"If I could afford a room, I wouldn't be standing here begging my heartless sister to take me in," Kendra said, her voice all soft and needy.

Kiley's eyes flashed with something, some kind of recognition tinged with anger. "Don't Kendra. Not here, and not him."

Rob wasn't real sure what was going on, but the air between the two sisters felt like shredded glass. "We don't charge family," he said. "I'll make a call." He picked up his phone from the coffee table and glanced at Kiley. "I'll go outside."

"No, Rob. We will." She swallowed hard. "And I'm sorry about all this." She grabbed her sister by the arm, and marched her into the kitchen and right out the door. But she didn't close it behind her. Instead she said, "Wait, here." Then she came back inside, pulled the door closed behind her, and walked right to him. "I didn't lie to you about Kendra. I thought she was dead."

"I got that."

She nodded. "Rob, no one can know she's alive. I don't know why she did what she did, but there had to be a reason. She's my sister. I have to protect her."

She was looking down, her hair falling in ribbons he wanted to touch. He put his hands on her shoulders and she lifted her head and looked him in the eyes. "It's not just you, is it? Your whole family is full of secrets and lies."

She held his gaze. There was naked honesty in her eyes. At least, that's what he thought he saw there. God knew it was what he wanted to see.

"We were not...nice people. I wanted a fresh start. I wanted to change, to become...different. But I didn't even know what that meant until I started spending time with you and your crazy family. But I feel like I'm doing it now. I'm becoming the person I want to be."

He held her blue eyes, his hands resting lightly on her hips. "That was real, wasn't it? That was your truth." She nodded. "I appreciate that you trusted me with it."

"I'm gonna need to trust you with a little bit more, Rob. She's gotta stay dead for now. Just until I figure out what she was hiding from, and what to do with her. If not, she's gonna be in a lot of trouble."

"I don't like dishonesty. I never even considered breaking the law."

"I'm not asking you to lie or commit a crime. Just...don't say anything. Just give me some time."

"I don't like lying, Kiley, and I'm not very good at it. But I want to trust you and I want you trust me back." He took a breath, made up his mind. "Yes. I'll keep your sister's secret for now. And I think I can convince my brothers to do the same if she takes a room at the saloon. Cause I'm not gonna lie to them about who she is, Kiley."

"I won't ask you to. And thanks. That's pretty amazing of you."

"You're welcome. Now maybe you can take a moment to realize you've just been given a miracle. Your sister is alive." He smiled at her. "She's alive, Kiley."

She smiled too. "Yeah. That's pretty amazing, isn't it?"

"It is." His eyes kind of got stuck in hers. At some point his arms had crept around her waist and he was holding her kind of close to him.

"So are you gonna kiss me or what?" she whispered.

He was still smiling when he answered by hugging her tighter, and covering her mouth with his. She tasted sweet, like he'd dreamed she would. And she kissed him back with just as much enthusiasm as he was feeling.

Enthusiasm, hell. He had unicorns dancing around in his brain, poking holes in his sanity.

Then she pulled free of him, sent him a long, lingering look as she backed across the kitchen to the door.

Rob watched her go through it, and she didn't close it behind her. The two sisters walked away out toward the barn.

His head was spinning. She wanted him, too. That made this whole thing way more serious, and therefore scary. But good scary. Roller coaster scary. He wanted to jump and click his heels, but since he wasn't a leprechaun, he just muttered, "Hot damn," and left it at that.

The rest...well, hell, the rest was a knot to be untangled. But she was starting to open up to him. And that made all the rest okay.

He called the saloon to see if his brothers could find Kendra a room.

~

Kendra shook a cigarette from a pack in her purse and lit up, blowing smoke into the night air as she paced away from the house.

It was dark, the wide sky full of stars, crickets singing like a chorus. The air was a warm kiss on Kiley's face. Rare thing, a humid night here. There was rain in the air.

"Place hasn't changed a bit, has it?" Kendra asked, rubbing her arms and looking around as if she'd missed it.

"What is this, Kendra?" Kiley stopped walking and tried again to swallow the lump in her throat. She didn't know what the heck had just happened between her and Rob, but it had felt very important. And she couldn't even bask in it, much less analyze it right now, because of Kendra.

She wanted to hug her sister again and weep for joy that she wasn't dead. But it would be kind of like hugging a porcupine and hoping not to get stabbed. So she stood there in front of the house where they'd lived together, grown up together, raised hell together, and she stared at her sister in the darkness. It felt like looking at a stranger. She was so cold, so hard.

"What do you *think* it is?" Kendra asked.

"I think you heard the place was being sold and came here to try to get your hands on it."

Kendra started walking away from the house and around toward the back. "Is the boulder still there, down by the river?"

"Where would it go?"

She shrugged, took another puff. The smoke made a little cloud around her head.

"Tell me why you came back," Kiley said.

"Same reason you did. I was homesick. I just...wanted to see the place again. I didn't expect you to be here."

"You didn't come to buy it?"

"With what?" She puffed, blew angrily, shook her head, her dead straight strawberry blond hair punctuating the motion. "I don't have enough to buy a fucking cup of coffee, Kiley. I'm broke, and I'm hungry and I'm homeless. And my own sister won't take me in. What the hell am I supposed to make of that?"

"You're lying." Kiley knew for a fact her sister had money. She'd stolen it from that oversized, lovesick Dax. She glanced at the car, a late model Prius and said, "You've got wheels."

"Borrowed."

"Has it been reported stolen yet?"

"Borrowed," Kendra said again. "God Kiley, you've changed. What are you, some kind of princess now? Big shot landowner? How'd you get the money to pay for the place, anyway? Or is he the one who bought it?"

"It's none of your business."

"What kind of game are you working here, sis?"

Kiley shook her head. "It's not a game."

"No?"

"No." She truly had changed, though, Kiley thought. She felt it like never before, maybe because of the stark contrast she could see between her and Kendra now that her sister was right there beside her. The pictures she'd been painting of her future life used to seem like impossible dreams. But she didn't see them that way anymore. They were goals now. She could get there.

Her sister was looking at her, waiting, so she tried to gather words to explain what was happening to her. "I'm trying to make a life here, Kendra. A normal life, like a normal person. I'm going to earn an honest living with this place."

"Sure you are. You and Mr. Moneybags in there, right? And

you just happened to partner up with the richest family in town?"

Kiley's body went cold. She stood very still and said, "How do you know anything about Rob or his family?"

She shrugged, puffed, blew more stinky smoke into the fresh night air. "Look, I don't care what kind of game you're running on him. I'm not gonna try to cut myself in and I'm not gonna mess it up. I got my own stuff going on. But I'm not leaving, either."

"Why? What the hell do you want here?"

One last puff, then she dropped the butt into the grass and crushed it with her heel. "I want to be with my loving family. You know, like a *normal* person." She smiled slowly, her eyes moving over Kiley's face, and there was a threat in them.

The screen door creaked. Kiley heard Rob's footsteps, soft in the grass. He came out a little ways, but not too far, and called, "Jason says the fella using my old room just checked out. It's yours if you want it, Kendra."

The dark look vanished and Kendra's smile was so bright it lit the darkness. She pivoted and walked quickly back to where Rob stood. "Thank you so much. I don't know what to say. I didn't know men like you still existed. She leaned up on tiptoe and kissed his jaw.

Kiley stood where she was, seething, but saying nothing. She felt like she'd grown roots.

"It's no problem," Rob said. But he took a sideways step away from her. "If you head back toward town—"

"I know where it is." She shot a quick look Kiley's way. "I saw it on the way out here. Hard to miss."

He nodded. "They're expecting you."

"I'll repay you, somehow." Then she hurried back to Kiley and hugged her hard.

Kiley stood stiffly, trembling. It hurt that the embrace was just a part of the picture Kendra was trying to paint for Rob's benefit. It wasn't real. Kendra didn't love her, didn't care about her. Probably wouldn't have bothered letting her know she was alive, if she didn't see some profit in showing up and revealing herself.

That was the part that worried her. What on earth did Kendra have to gain by showing up here in Big Falls now?

Kendra stopped hugging and took a step back, her face cold and hard, her back to Rob. "I'll see you soon, okay?"

There was a chill in those words. Then she plastered her big, fake smile on, turned around and walked quickly back to her car. A few minutes later, she was backing out of the driveway, turning and heading down the road.

Rob came closer. Kiley couldn't seem to move. She just stood there, watching the two red taillights fade in the distance, completely shocked.

He came up to her, put his hands on her shoulders, rubbed them up and down a little. "Are you okay?"

She forced herself to stop gazing sightlessly into the darkness, shifted to meet his eyes, and was struck again by how kind they were. And how beautiful. They were the brown of dark chocolate. "She's bad news, Rob. She's very bad news. You shouldn't have put her anywhere near your family."

He lifted a hand as if to touch her. "My family knows a beautiful con when they see one."

"They do?"

"*We* do. We're decent looking, rich, and single. You think she's gonna be the first?"

She blinked fast, shook her head.

"Did you think you were?"

"Robby, that's not...that's not who I am. Not anymore."

"I know that. I wouldn't be here if I didn't."

She lowered her head, saw the cigarette butt in the grass, felt dirty and polluted. Crouching, she picked it up. "I'm not proud of my past, Rob. I haven't been...a good person. I've done things, illegal things. But I want to change. I'm...I'm trying to change."

He nodded. "You've already changed," he said. "Look, maybe I don't know who you've been. But I think I know who you are."

She shook her head.

"You're Kiley Kellogg, co-owner of the Holiday Ranch of Big Falls, Oklahoma. Entrepreneur and all-around good person. And you need to get some sleep. We've got a big day tomorrow."

"You're not angry?"

"About what?"

"Dragging you into this mess with my sister?"

"I might've been. But that kiss in the kitchen kind of melted me into a puddle at your feet." His fingers threaded into her hair, and he leaned in a little bit.

"I thought I was the one melting," she whispered. She felt the pull of him, the way her body swayed closer as if drawn by his gravity. He kissed her, just a soft brush of his impossibly soft lips over hers. Then he straightened away, took her hand, and tugged her further away from the house, all the way out toward the end of the driveway. He clasped her shoulders, turned her to face the house and said, "Notice anything different?"

"It's dark outside, Rob. How am I gonna notice—"

"Wait right here. Do not move from this spot." Then he ran inside. She heard his feet pounding up the stairs and frowned, wondering what he was up to. Then suddenly, the attic light came on, and its stained glass window came to life.

He came running back out about the time her tears made those jewel toned light beams turn liquid. "How did you...where was...my God, Rob, it's beautiful."

"Found it in the attic. Thought I'd surprise you by getting it fixed and..." He stopped and stared down at her. "I didn't mean to make you cry."

She flung her arms around his neck and hugged him. "Thank

you. Thank you, Rob. I don't...I don't know how I wound up here with you. How I deserve...you're just amazing."

"Glad you think so." He held her against him, one hand stroking her hair. "If finding things in the attic earns me this kind of gratitude, maybe I should mention that I also found a boxful of little girl books, an old guitar, and—"

"*Guitar*? You found my old guitar too?" She let go of him and ran into the house, straight through, up the stairs and into the bedroom closet. In a flash she'd tugged down the stairs and was in the attic, looking around at all the stuff.

"Over there," Rob said. He was partway up the ladder, and he pointed.

She ran to the corner, picked up the case, brushed off the dust. "The case has a tortoiseshell pattern to it under all this grime. I wonder if the guitar's still okay?"

"The place has been warm and dry, I don't know why it wouldn't be." He nodded at her to proceed.

Biting her lip, Kiley flipped the latches and opened the hard-shell case. Inside, her precious Gibson still gleamed. She took it out and cradled it in her arms. "I didn't have the chance to take it with me."

"It's special to you."

She nodded. "It was my mother's. It's the only thing of hers I had. Until I got her ranch back."

"You didn't have an easy start in life, did you, Kiley?"

"Does anybody, really?"

He shrugged. She adjusted her grip on the instrument, brushed her thumb across the strings, and made a face at the discordant sounds they made. "Probably needs all new strings." She replaced the guitar in the case, and closed the lid. "I really like you, Rob. A lot."

He smiled. "I like you back."

"I don't want to screw up our business stuff," she said.

"I don't want that either. But at the same time, I don't want to pass up what could be...something important. Something special."

"You think this might be...something like that?"

"I'm thinking it might be, yeah."

Her smile was impossible to tame. "I'm glad I'm not the only one."

He came the rest of the way up, crossed the attic. She stood up when he got to her. "So we take it kind of slow, and careful."

"Like normal people do," she said.

He kissed her, like she'd been waiting for him to, and for a little while, they stood there, making out in the dusty attic, and she felt like a teenager with her first crush.

No. This was bigger. *Way* bigger than a crush.

And finally, he pulled away gently. "Slow and careful."

"Within reason," she said.

# CHAPTER TEN

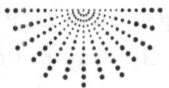

Saturday morning came far too early. She'd barely slept. There was something restless inside her, something nervous, and excited and overjoyed and terrified, all at the same time. And she knew it was all about Rob and her, and those kisses they'd shared yesterday, and her deep down certainty that she didn't deserve him.

But she wanted to. She wanted to be the kind of woman a man like Rob could be with. Could...love, maybe.

Her fear came from wondering if she was up to the challenge.

On top of that, she was sure her sister was up to something. And it probably involved one of the McIntyres. They were the most prime hunks of eligible in town, and Kendra had wormed her way right into the middle of them. Damn, she was good.

Kiley grabbed her things and slipped through the silent hall, to the bathroom. Either she was up too early, or not quite early enough.

Quick as she could manage it, she stood under the steamy spray. As she let the hot water sooth her, she tried to sort through the cyclone of feelings swirling around inside.

Kendra was alive. She hadn't died a horrible, painful death. Kiley was relieved and overjoyed. And yet she was furious at Kendra for deliberately letting her grieve for nearly two months.

Kendra was dangerous.

Kiley would just have to handle her. She knew Kendra, and she knew all her tricks. Their father had raised them together, side by side, and he'd taught them together, too. Just because she hadn't taken to the trade the way Kendra had, that didn't mean Kiley didn't know. She knew everything.

From the moment she'd learned Kendra was alive, all Kiley had thought about was protecting her sister. But suddenly she knew with sparkling clarity that she had to protect Rob's family and all of Big Falls *from* Kendra. She *had* to.

She got out of the shower, towel dried her hair and combed it back into a smooth ponytail. Looking into the mirror, she found herself kissing Rob again in her mind. She closed her eyes and felt his mouth on hers. The way he moved his soft, thick lips, just a little, like a caress.

She nodded to herself, and said, "I'll fix this, Robby. I'll find out what she's up to and send her packing. I will. You'll see."

She was pretty sure she could do it and still keep her sister from being caught or arrested for faking her own death. She could do both.

She closed her eyes and thought about kissing Rob again. And then something occurred to her and she straightened her head and stared bug-eyed at herself. What if she loved him or something? And what if he found out about her life and her past and all the crap she'd done, and just bailed? That would *hurt*.

Her stomach in knots, she dressed in jeans, with a white tank top and a lightweight cotton shirt over it to protect her arms from slivers and the sun. When she stepped out of the bathroom, she could already hear the voices of Rob's family, all talking at once outside the house. Trucks were coming and going, and oh, yes, she smelled coffee.

She took a deep breath, told herself to relax. This was all just part of her transformation. She'd kind of thought it would be easy, but now that seemed kind of naive. The smell of the coffee was a balm. She took it in and trotted down the stairs.

Vidalia stood in the kitchen, her long raven curls spilling out around a green bandana. She was just filling a big yellow mug with the precious brew. She had big brown doe eyes and tanned skin and she was ageless. Kiley wanted to *be* her when she got old.

Vidalia caught her eye, smiled brightly, and held out the mug. "I heard the shower stop. By God, you must be about ready to shoot us all, milling around here all the time like we own the place."

Kiley smiled back and took the mug. "I never shoot anyone who gives me coffee," she said.

"That's why I made it. Sheer self-preservation." She laughed, then sipped. "The guys are all out in the bigger barn already."

Rob's plan was to hoe the barn out and build stables for his first bunch of horses.

"I knew he wanted to get an early start. I just didn't know how early," she said, then she sipped gratefully. "Good coffee."

"Arabica beans. I ground them up fresh."

"You brought your own coffee?"

"Coffee is sacred. I didn't know what you had in the cupboard, so…"

"So Miz Vidalia is a coffee snob!" Kiley said. Then she held her breath and wondered if she'd gone too far.

Vidalia glared at her. Then she slapped her thigh and laughed out loud. "You got me. I am."

"I, too, appreciate a good cup of coffee." She took another sip of the really excellent brew. "There's a lot of junk packed into that barn. I should get out there and help."

"Not without a decent breakfast to shore you up. Sit down, Kiley. I've been wanting to have some time to get to know you better."

Kiley saw the friendly light in Vidalia's eyes and sat down.

"My husband tells me your sister's in town."

"You know?" Kiley closed her eyes, shook her head and said, "Of course you know. Bobby Joe owns the saloon, she's staying at the saloon, hence, you know."

"We're not real big on keeping secrets from each other in this family," she said. But Robby asked us not to tell anyone else that she's in town. He didn't tell us why."

"I'm afraid I can't either. She's... she's my sister. I need to try to help her."

Vidalia nodded. "I understand protecting family." Her eyes were loaded with meaning.

"Rob said...he said since we're partners, I should consider you all family." She spoke slowly, chose her words carefully. "And I'm honored by that. I've never seen a family I'd love to be a part of more. I want you to know, I intend to live up to it."

"Do you, now?" Vidalia's gaze sharpened, and she seemed to look her over way more thoroughly than was comfortable.

Then with a tilt of her head and an arch of her brows, she went back to the counter, grabbed a plate filled with scrambled eggs and hash browns, and set it in front of Kiley. She took a seat opposite her and slid a large, flat book across to her. "I got this for you."

It was a Big Falls Central School Yearbook. She opened it up to a page marked with a playing card and tapped the photo.

Kiley looked down at her own face and her twin sister's. Sixth grade and thinking everything would always be just the way it was then.

"Where did you go after that, Kiley?"

"We...we moved east. Dad...couldn't afford to keep the

place. It was never a working ranch, not in my memory anyway. My mother inherited it."

"So your dad moved you east?"

Kiley nodded, sipped her coffee to avoid having to say more than that. Then she set her cup down. "It was really nice of the family to let my sister stay at the saloon," she said, and mentally she was trying to figure out how to warn Vidalia without admitting that she was a criminal raised by a family of criminals.

"I was surprised you didn't want her to stay here at the ranch," she said. "Seeing that she grew up here."

"Vidalia...you're a smart woman."

"One of the perks of age. There are precious few, but wisdom is a big one."

She was trying to put her at ease, Kiley realized. She took a deep breath. "My sister...she's um...."

"She's a man-eater," Vidalia said, matter of factly. "I went over to clean up the room, make sure she had everything she needed. Met her. She might be foolin' the boys, but she's not foolin' me."

"I'm...a little worried about Jason and Joey."

"I appreciate the warning. I'll keep an eye on things."

Kiley nodded. "While she's here, we're gonna refer to her as Kendra Jones, my cousin from back east."

Vidalia sat back in her chair. "Is she wanted by the law?"

"I don't know, exactly. I need to find out."

Vidalia nodded. "What are you gonna do?"

She took a deep breath and said, "Honestly, Vidalia, I don't know yet. But my goal is to get her out of this town. I just need to make sure she'll be safe when she leaves."

She lifted a forefinger. "If you need help, come to me. Don't wait until it's too late to prevent the damage. All right?"

"I promise."

Vidalia searched her eyes for a minute, then reached into her purse and pulled out her cell phone. "What's your mobile number?" she asked.

The change of topic threw her, but after a second, she managed to spit out her digits while Vidalia tapped her phone. "There," she said. "You've been added to the family's group text lists. There's one for just the women, and another for everyone. The guys have a men-only group, but they don't think we know about it. Now finish up your food. We've got lots to do."

Feeling as if she'd just experienced a Brand-McIntyre rite-of-passage, Kiley ate.

She didn't think she'd ever worked as hard in her life as she did that day. The big barn had a lot of stuff inside. When she'd lived there, it had been deemed off limits by her dad, and though she and Kendra had sneaked out there quite often, all Kiley had ever noticed were broken boards and hulking metal pieces of rusted-out farm equipment.

By noon, Jason, Joey, Rob, and their father, Bobby Joe, had emptied every ounce of junk from that big barn. It was all in front of the building where Kiley and Vidalia sorted it into piles. More family had shown up—Vidalia's sons-in-law. Wade had driven a big red tow-truck over, with ARMSTRONG painted on the side.

The men were all inside the barn building stalls. The smell of fresh-cut lumber filled the air, and the sounds of power tools and hammers were outshouting the birds.

Outside, she and Vidalia continued to pick through relics. Tall milk cans from days gone by, wooden crates piled full of tools, the likes of which she'd never seen before, with hand cranks and wooden handles. There was a box full of hurricane lamps, most of them with intact globes. There were old tin signs for businesses that no longer existed, Big Falls Livery & Tack. Fanny Mae's Soda Fountain, and one that just said BLACKSMITH in block letters on an oval piece of metal with two holes in the top for hooks. "I bet Jason would like this," Kiley said, holding the sign up. "Rob said he lives in what was once a blacksmith's shop."

Vidalia looked at it and smiled hugely. "He'd love it. That's such a great idea, Kiley."

"I'll put it away. We can surprise him for his birthday or something." Kiley wiped her forehead and looked around at the piles. "What are we gonna do with all the rest of this? Is the local dump still open?"

"Sure, but these things are worth some money." Vidalia paused, too, in her work, and waved Kiley over to a shady spot underneath a gnarled old tree. "I think what you've got here is a windfall, hon." She poured a glass of sweet tea from the large pitcher and handed it to Kiley. They'd set up an inverted wooden box to hold the tea and Solo cups, and two others to sit on.

"Really?" Kiley took the tea and a seat.

Vidalia filled a second cup and sat down beside her, fanning her face with a big woven fan that looked like a giant leaf. "I have a friend in antiques. Let me give him a call. Maybe he'd handle selling them for you for a small commission. Unless you want to do it yourself. You could take photos, list them online—"

"No, no, I'd be grateful for your friend's help. I wouldn't even know what to ask for them."

"Good."

"You know, there's more stuff piled up in the small barn," Kiley said with a nod in that direction.

Vidalia looked that way with interest. "Oh, we *have* to take a look."

They worked the entire morning, and when lunchtime

rolled around, Maya and the twins showed up with a car full of food.

They sat on upturned plastic buckets and old wooden crates, around a picnic table made from an old barn door laid out across a pair of saw horses. The whole family was talking, mostly all at once, and somehow it was contagious. Kiley found herself telling Rob excitedly about the barn's treasures and Vidalia's notion that they might be worth some bucks, and he was smiling with his whole heart as he listened.

"Speaking of bucks," Wade said. Then he nodded toward the old car they'd pulled out of the barn. It was hooked to his tow-truck, its front end in the air like a rearing stallion. "I know the idea was to fix that baby up for you to drive, but it's kind of a classic," he said. "I'm wondering if you'd consider selling it to me."

Kiley looked at Rob, then at the old, rust-colored vehicle. "Seriously?"

"It would make a great project car."

"Are you sure you're not just trying to help out a broke girl?" she asked with a smile. "Cause you guys have really done enough."

Wade grinned at her. "You won't think that after you see what I'm gonna do with it. Actually, I've got a ten-year-old Wrangler at the shop I've been trying to sell. I took it in place of cash for some work I did last year, and it's still sitting there. Runs great, moderate mileage. How about a trade?"

She frowned and looked from Wade to Rob. "That wouldn't be fair. The El Camino is half Rob's."

"It'll be fair enough if you let me drive it from time to time," Rob said. "I've seen this Wrangler. Take the deal."

She smiled at him, and her heart got all bouncy and happy again. "Okay, I'll take the deal."

"Sweet," Wade said. He reached across the table to shake on it.

"We need to hoe out that smaller barn next," Rob said.

"Vidalia and I are gonna poke around in there after lunch."

"What are your plans for the smaller barn?" Bobby Joe asked.

"It'll be a haunted house in the fall," Kiley said. "Next year I'm gonna grow pumpkins and a corn maze. This year we'll have to settle for the spook house and hayrides. We just have time to get it ready, too. And if the antiques sell like Vidalia thinks they will, I'll have some money to fund it." She glanced Rob's way. "With my half, I mean."

Bobby Joe sent Rob a loaded look. Rob held up a hand. "I know, Dad. I know." Then he said, "Kiley, I can't take half the proceeds from the antiques."

"Why not? They're half yours."

"May I say something?" Bobby Joe asked.

Joey said, "Since when do you ask first, Dad?"

"Since never." He set down a big yellow ear of sweet corn and said, "Robert, imagine for a moment you make a great success of this horse ranch of yours."

"He's absolutely going to," Vidalia said.

"I have no doubt. So let's say you do. You raise beautiful thoroughbreds."

"Quarter Horses," Rob corrected.

"One day you get married." Every single one of them looked at Kiley when he said that, and she felt heat flood her face. But Bobby Joe kept right on talking. "And you have a son. And you raise him up, and you work together on the ranch. By your side, he learns how to run it, how to raise horses. And then one day, you decide you want to retire. And you say to him, 'son, this beautiful place, this business I've built with my own two hands, it's all yours now.' And he says to you, 'No, thanks. I don't want it.'"

Rob picked up a napkin and wiped his mouth.

"You'd be hurt, that's what," Vidalia said. "Cut right to the quick. You'd feel like your life's work had been judged and found lacking. You'd feel like the gift you worked so hard to give your son had been rejected, thrown right back in your face. And you would bleed, Robby. You would bleed just the way your father bleeds when you refuse to use the resources he worked so hard to provide for you. You act like his wealth is something dirty."

"It's not like that. Dad, come on, you know it's not like that."

"I do. I know. You just want to make it on your own."

"Exactly."

"I'm just starting to wonder what I did it all for. Was my life's work a waste of time? You won't touch a dime. Jason is pretty much doing the same," he added with a look at his eldest son.

"I'll take their shares," Joey said, grinning.

Everyone rolled their eyes at him. He just shrugged and took another bite of his hot dog.

Rob pushed his plate away and he looked at Kiley. "What do you think about all this?"

She blinked at him, shocked to her core that he'd want to know her opinion on it. "I understand how you feel, Rob. I kind of chose to reject my dad's line of work too." She shrugged then. "I understand how you feel too, Mr. McIntyre."

"Bobby Joe," the man corrected.

"Bobby Joe. But really, I don't know why it has to be such a big problem. The solution's obvious enough to me."

Everyone stopped eating. They were riveted, even Joey set down the final two inches of his hot dog bun.

"Well, spit it out girl. Don't keep us in suspense," Vidalia said.

"Yes, spit it out, girl," Rob repeated.

She smiled at him, because he'd used Vidalia's exact inflection. "Use the money your dad put aside for you like a loan. Get yourself up and running, and then when the ranch starts showing a profit, pay it all back with interest. Sock it away someplace and then later, when that someday comes and you have a kid, you can pass it and all the guilt that goes with it right on to him. Or her. And if they do the same, and their kids do the same, your whole family will always have access to a fortune to fund all their dreams and projects, forever and ever. Amen." She took a drink from the beer on the table and set it down. "It's not rocket science."

"No, it's sure as hell not," Rob said, gazing at her like she was wearing a halo.

"Watch the language, Robby." Vidalia picked up her water and tilted it Kiley's way. "Here's to you, girl. You're wise beyond your years."

A car came rolling in a dust cloud up the driveway. Kiley's stomach tied itself up in knots as soon as she saw who it was. Kendra got out. Tight jeans, cowboy boots, even a hat. Oh, she was trying to play the part, wasn't she? To worm her way into this family.

"Hey, nobody told me there was a party," she said, smiling bright and avoiding Kiley's eyes. She came right to the table and found a spot next to Joey, who looked like he grew a foot taller as soon as she sat down.

No, Kiley thought. Not Joey.

~

Joey and Kendra left together when the day's work was done. Kiley watched them go with a knot in her stomach the size of a grapefruit.

"I talked to him. Told him to watch his back," Rob said. "He'll be all right."

He wouldn't. Kiley knew he wouldn't. She kept thinking about Dax, the big jerk, and how much trouble he was in over her sister. Kendra had destroyed the guy. She'd do the same to Joey. He didn't stand a chance.

"Where are they going?" she asked.

"He's taking her to dinner in Tucker Lake. Probably Haggerty House. It's the best restaurant around. You ever been?"

She shook her head. "Dad wasn't much for taking rowdy girls out to fancy restaurants," she said.

"Your dad. He's ... away, you said?"

She lowered her head. Her dad was in prison. Why didn't she just tell him? It wouldn't take a lot of digging for him to find out.

But maybe she wouldn't have to. Maybe she could convince her sister to get out of town and leave Joey alone.

"I can't believe your family. The way they pitched in."

"I'm still getting used to it myself." She frowned at him. He smiled back, hauled the barn door open and then they walked side by side into it. "It's the Brands," he said. "I mean, yeah, my brothers would help me out anytime, but when Dad married Vidalia, we inherited her entire clan. Wade's a freaking genius."

"With cars and motors, you mean?"

"With lots of things. He wired the whole barn today. Look at this." He threw a switch and the lights came on. "The guy's gifted."

Kiley looked down the length of the barn. Wooden stalls lined either side, ending about halfway down, and they smelled of fresh-cut lumber. "When will you start bringing in horses?"

He shrugged. "Just as soon as I get the fences up. They're gonna need places to graze."

"Which could probably get done in a couple of days, with all the help you have."

He nodded, averted his eyes.

"I saw that," she said. "Something's holding you back."

He met her eyes again. "I really don't want my father's money. I want to do it on my own."

"And you don't like my suggestion? To use it like a bank loan, and then pay it all back? And leave it to grow and then give it all to your kids someday?"

"What would you do?"

"I'm no expert on money, Rob."

"You're no slouch at it. You managed to wrangle a pile of it in cash to pay for your half of the ranch."

She lowered her eyes. "I've gotta pay all of that back." He waited for her to say more, but she didn't want to, so she changed the subject. "Why are you so against using the resources you've had handed to you?"

He lowered his head, then lifted it again and looked her in the eye, nodded once. "You know what? I'm gonna tell you."

He slung an arm around her shoulders, casual, friendly, but still being that close to him made her go warm right to her toes. He led her out the back door of the barn, flicking off the lights on the way, and then they walked together along the twisting trail that led down to the river. At the riverbank, he dropped his arm to his side, so she hopped up onto the boulder. He stood at the water's edge and pitched a couple of flat stones, skipping them impressively.

"I was almost engaged just a little over a year ago."

She felt her jaw drop, then quickly clamped it shut again.

He picked up another stone. "We'd been seeing each other for seven months. She lived two hundred miles from me, but I thought we were making it work. Managed to have at least one night a week together. Long distance relationship. I wanted more. So I decided to pop the question. To me it was obvious that's where things were heading. I planned it all out, bought the ring, the whole nine. Got down on one knee, pulled that little black box outta my pocket and she looked at me like her eyes were gonna pop."

"She was surprised?"

"She was horrified. And then she told me she was already married."

"Oh no," Kiley whispered.

"She said that she'd never meant to give me the idea she was serious about me. She said she'd considered leaving her husband for me once, early on, but the minute I told her my feelings about my father's money, about wanting to make it on my own, she knew she never would. Her husband was a wealthy man. She liked being a wealthy woman. My family fortune was what drew her to me in the first place, she said. And then she liked me too much to break it off when she found out I didn't plan to touch it." He paused there for a moment, skipped another rock. "I decided then that I would make my own way, and that I'd tell women up front, you know if I ever got involved again."

"That way you'd know if they were interested in you, or your money." Kiley slid off the boulder to land on her feet in the grass, and walked up behind him. She didn't mean to slide her hands up to his shoulders. It just happened. And she said, "That chick was out of her freakin' mind, Robby. You're worth so much more than money."

He glanced down at her. "I wasn't angling for pity."

"That's good, cause you're not getting any. It was a lucky break, she said no. What if you'd married her and *then* found out what she was like?"

He grinned. "Since when are you the one who finds the silver lining?"

"Since I came back here. Since I came...home." She took a deep breath and turned to look around her. Tall yellow grasses moved with every breeze, making the fields look like a rippling, golden lake. "I didn't realize how much I missed it 'til I came back. There's somethin' about this place...."

"Yeah, there is. Vidalia says it's magic. Says Big Falls chooses the people who belong here, and casts its spell on them so they never want to leave."

"I almost believe that." She sighed. "I wonder if it's capable of spitting out the ones who don't belong here and making them never want to come back."

"You're thinking about your sister now."

She nodded. "She's trouble, Rob. I love her, but she hurts people." And then she lowered her head. "I haven't always been much different."

"But you are now."

She lifted her head. "I am." She looked up and found him staring down at her.

He lifted a hand to push her hair off her forehead, and his eyes locked onto hers. "I'm going to use the trust fund to pay for the mares and get my business started. But I'm paying every penny back."

"Why are you telling me that?"

"So you know it up front. I'm not a billionaire. And I don't ever want to be. I'm just a gentleman cowboy with a good credit score. Okay?"

She frowned at him, wondering why he'd even asked. "It's fine with me."

"Good. Now I have two questions for you."

Kiley wondered if he was going to ask her about her own past now. She might have to tell him something. He'd shared his painful past with her, and fair was fair.

"Is it okay with you if we do the same with your end of the business?" he asked.

She blinked. "The same what?" And then she got his meaning.

"We spend what we need to get it up and running from my funds, and we pay it back once we're turning a profit."

She took a step back from him, shaking her head. It was exactly what she would have been planning if she had chosen him as a mark. She'd get him to fall for her and pay for everything, and eventually she'd figure a way to buy him out for next to nothing, and send him packing.

Was this some kind of test? Was fate playing games with her, to see if she was really serious?

"Well?"

She lifted her eyes to his, met them, held them. "I don't want you to be offended, but I can't. And I don't want you to ask me why or try to talk me into anything. I just plain can't."

He thinned his lips, but he nodded.

"Caleb offered me a job in the law office. I have two weeks to decide. So I can use that to get my end of the biz up and running if I have to."

"Okay. If that's what you have to do."

"It is."

God, that felt good. She sighed in relief and felt lighter, an involuntary smile tugged at her lips. "What was your second question?"

"Way more important, actually," he said. "I'd very much like to kiss you again. Would that be okay with you?"

"More than okay." She answered too fast, almost before he finished talking, and the words came out kind of croaky and hoarse.

She blinked up at him, and he smiled, then slowly curled his arms around her waist, and lowered his head. She let her eyes fall closed as his lips met hers. Then she curled her arms around his neck and stood on tiptoe to get a little closer. His lips nudged hers apart, and the sweetness that was filling her veins turned molten. He hugged her tighter, held her closer, kissed her more deeply. Her heart started pounding in her ears, and then she started shaking.

He lifted his head away, smiling down into her eyes.

"I hardly know what to do here," she said.

"You don't have to do anything. There's nothing either of us have to do. We're gonna take things as they come. Nice and easy. No pressure, no hurry. I just...I need honesty."

She nodded. "I get that. And I don't blame you. I just... I still need time."

He looked right into her eyes. "Just don't let me fall too hard before you hit me with a deep dark secret that's gonna ruin it, okay?"

She blinked at him, stunned because it was almost like he was predicting the future. "Okay."

"Okay. Come on inside. We'll hit the net and I'll show you the mares I've got my eye on." He put his arm around her again, and they walked back toward the house.

Things were good. Things were so, so good. She could make it here. She could be the kind of woman a man like Rob McIntyre deserved. She could build a business, earn her money honestly, pay back the people she'd wronged. She could make a life she was proud of.

Unless her sister ruined it all.

# CHAPTER ELEVEN

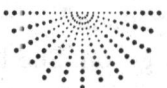

iley came down from her morning shower looking cool and pretty in a pair of pink shorts and a sleeveless white button-down blouse. She'd pulled her still-damp hair back into a ponytail that was curling as it dried. But her eyes looked sleepy.

Rob was already up, had made the coffee, and filled her a mugful when he heard her coming down the stairs. "Good morning, beautiful."

"Ha. I look like I've been rode hard and put away wet." She bit her lip, took the mug. "That's a horse-related saying, not a sex-related saying."

He laughed softly and leaned back against the counter. She sipped her coffee, and he saw her noticing that he'd fixed it the way she liked it, with an overdose of cream and sugar. "So you didn't sleep well?"

"Tossed and turned all night, in spite of the brand new bed. I keep thinking about the people I've hurt, the people my sister's hurt—"

He liked the sounds of that. "You have a conscience."

"I know." she admitted it as guiltily as if he'd said, "You have bad breath."

"A conscience is a good thing, Kiley."

"Not when you've done the things I have. And my sister—"

"You're not responsible for cleaning up her messes. They're not your doing."

She sighed and said, "I can clean up one of her messes, though. One I helped perpetuate."

He waited for her to go on. She looked at him for a long moment, and then sighed heavily and said, "Okay here it is. I'm gonna tell you. That guy, Dax Russell? The one who was looking for me?"

He nodded. "He was actually looking for your sister, though. That was her photo he was showing around."

"Yeah." She took a deep breath. "I got his contact info and called him. We met at a little café in Tucker Lake yesterday."

"*Alone?*" He almost barked the word, then held up a hand and said, "Sorry. Go on."

"He showed me the photo. Told me it was taken a couple of weeks ago. I told him she was dead, and it about broke his big old heart."

"I wouldn't worry too much about his big old heart, hon."

"He had tears in his eyes, Rob. I think he's actually a decent guy. And then I came back and there she was, alive and well."

"And you think you need to track him down? Tell him the truth?"

"I don't know. I don't know yet what she's running from. But I think he can be trusted. At the very least, I have to try to get his money back for him. She conned him out of a bundle. Told him it was for a kidney transplant."

"He um...he was in love with her?"

"I think so. And he borrowed the money from the race track he runs for his father. She told him she'd have it back to him in just a couple of days. He's a nice guy, he really is. His father's gonna find out and he'll lose his job, and he just...he doesn't deserve all that."

He nodded. "So what do you want to do?"

She looked him in the eye. "I want to get into her room at The Long Branch. See if I can find Dax's money or anything that'll tell me what the hell she's running from and what she's up to in Big Falls."

He blinked, thought of something, and couldn't believe he'd thought of it. It was devious, and sly, and dishonest, and totally not him. And then he said it out loud. "It's Sunday."

"So?"

He told himself to shut up and kept talking anyway. "Sundays are gigantic, high-calorie combination lunch-dinners out at Dad and Vidalia's place. Right after church, which Vidalia never misses. She cooks enough to feed an army, which is fortunate because we are the size of one. The whole family's invited, and this week that includes you and your sister."

"Oh my God. Rob, I don't think she should be there. She's wrapping her tentacles around your family and—"

"And therefore will not be in her room this afternoon. And the saloon will be empty."

She looked at him like he'd sprouted horns. "You mean, you'd let me into her room?"

He tilted his head. "She has the only key. I lost mine while I was living there, had to take the extra one, and as far as I know, no one's had another copy made yet. So we'd have to...sort of... break in. Somehow."

"Shoot, I can pick that lock in under ten seconds," she said. Then she widened her eyes and clapped a hand over her mouth.

It's okay, he told himself. She's a *reformed* master criminal. Sort of.

"The guys are coming out to help me build fence this morning," he said, to get them off the subject of breaking and entering. Even though, technically he was part owner of what they were breaking into.

"Did you do it? Did you buy the mares?"

"Thanks to you, I did. They're coming this week." He was as excited about that as a kid a few days from summer vacation. He had been ever since he'd made the decision to use his father's money. The way she smiled, he got the feeling Kiley was excited, too.

"That's gonna be amazing." Her smile froze, then wavered and died.

"What? What's wrong?" he asked.

She heaved a big sigh, sipped more coffee. "I feel so lucky right now. To be here, in this place, with you. It's like life gave me a do-over."

"And that's a *good* thing."

"Unless I screw it up. I've got so much more to lose now than I had before. The beginning of a whole new life. A whole new me."

He went to her, took her cup away, slid his hands around her waist, and leaned down to kiss the tip of her nose. "You can't screw it up. You can only keep moving forward, one step at a time, making your life better and better with every one you take."

"And yet I'm starting to tangle you up in my family drama. And it's not you, Rob."

"You let me worry about what's me and what's not, okay?" Then reluctantly, he stepped away from her. "I've gotta get busy. I'll have Jason and Joey make our excuses to Vidalia for not making the big meal today. We'll probably have to promise to show up next week, though."

"Okay," she said.

She walked him to the front door. He stood there a second, and then figured what the hell, and swept her into his arms for a big kiss that reassured him he was doing the right thing. Even though he was also doing everything he'd sworn not to do. And he just wasn't thinking about the breaking and entering, either, but about letting himself fall for a women with a heart full of secrets.

Yet, he didn't feel as if he had much of a choice in the matter. And she was trying to turn over a new leaf. She hadn't told him everything. Not yet. But it was a start.

A good start, he hoped.

Kiley spent the morning pulling one item after another out of the smaller barn and stacking them outside. She uncovered an old fish tank she figured was worthless, but there was a very old-fashioned wooden high chair she thought had to be valuable. This stuff wasn't junk at all and never had been.

It was funny how her father had spent all his time here running various games and cons on people to get money, never even taking advantage of the treasure trove right under his nose.

And the ranch itself could bring in money. And would!

By mid-afternoon she was dirty and dusty, but the barn was empty, and she thought there were as many antiques in it as there had been in the larger one. She'd unearthed an old butter churn, several unbroken brown & tan crocks, three old-fashioned flat irons that were actually made of iron with wooden grips fastened onto their handles, and dozens of other treasures. She'd piled them all out in front of the barn with the things from the larger barn to await Vidalia's friend the antique dealer.

After a quick shower she put on fresh clothes—narrow, ankle-length jeans and a sleeveless, cotton button-down shirt in a pretty blue that matched her eyes. Yes, she was trying to look pretty. And yes, it was because Rob was going with her.

And he noticed. She felt him near, and then heard a little low wolf whistle, that had her grinning like an idiot as she pivoted to face him. He stood just inside the kitchen door, his T-shirt damp, a fine sheen on his forehead, hayseed sticking to his arms, and his cowboy hat still in place.

"You look too good to be in the same room with me, Kiley."

She had to lower her head to hide her burning cheeks. "I think the same about you every time I look at you," she said. She moved closer, but he held up both hands. "Don't get too close. I'm a mess. The guys just left. We've got the meadow out behind the barn completely fenced in and ready for the mares. I need a quick shower and then we can head out on our…secret mission."

"Yeah, about that…"

"What?" he asked. "You change your mind?" He sounded kind of hopeful.

"Not about breaking in. Only about dragging you with me to do it. A life of crime is not your thing, Rob. You're honest. This is gonna be bad for you."

"It's not really breaking in. I own the place. And your sister… well, frankly, she's a criminal and she's on the lam. The only thing I'm feeling morally ambiguous about is not just telling Jimmy about her and—"

"But he'd arrest her!" She stared at him wide-eyed. "He'd have to, he's the police chief."

"I know he would. But Kiley, have you thought maybe that would be the best thing for her? That she might learn something from it?"

"It would kill her, not reform her."

"It would keep her from victimizing anyone else."

She lowered her head. "She'd blame me."

"Well, who cares? What can she do to you from behind bars?"

"Offer testimony in exchange for a lighter sentence, maybe."

"Testimony against who?" Then he frowned hard. "You?"

She took a deep breath. "I've found my way without doing time. She can too, I know she can. I just need to find out what she's up to and put a stop to it, and get her the hell out of town before she gets caught and drags me down with her."

Rob sighed heavily. "Are you ever gonna tell me what you did?"

"Yes. I am."

"You are?" He looked up, surprised.

"Soon. This isn't the time. I need to get into her room while she's out at Vidalia and your dad's. But yes, I'm gonna tell you. Everything. I decided last night, while tossing and turning and mulling on my life and my mistakes and my decision to be better."

"I'm really glad to hear that," he said. "Give me five minutes to take a shower and we'll head over."

"If you're sure."

"I am."

"Okay, go shower. That'll give me time to dig my kit out of the trunk. It's buried in there somewhere."

"Your kit?" he asked, turning to head for the stairs.

"My lock picking kit." He turned around at those words, and she closed her eyes and said, "I should probably throw it away after this."

He smiled at her like you smile at particularly adorable puppy, but there was worry behind his eyes. Then he headed upstairs for his shower.

Rob drove them out past The Long Branch, then turned onto a dirt road, and parked where his truck would be out of sight. Then they both got out, but when he started walking down the road, Kiley grabbed his hand and said, "Let's cut through the woods. Take a look at the place from across the street, make sure it's empty."

He nodded, and followed her into the scrubby woodlot, hating to think that she knew what she was doing. But she did. Could he handle it? Oh, he'd already pegged her for a smalltime con. But what she'd admitted to him this morning had shaken him. She'd done things worthy of prison time. That was way more than he'd bargained for.

Now that she was on the brink of telling him everything, Rob wasn't sure he wanted to know.

No. He definitely wanted to know. He just wasn't sure if he could handle knowing.

She walked through the woods, kicking up the scents of the loblolly pines and undergrowth. They followed a sunlight dappled animal trail to the spot right across the street from the saloon and took a seat on a fallen log that smelled of earth and rotting bark.

He sat down beside her and watched her staring intently across the road at his family's saloon. She was in some kind of state of ultra focus. And she was as beautiful as always, but the sweetness wasn't there. She was on alert.

"Her car's still there," she said.

He dragged his eyes off her face and looked across the street. "Maybe she rode over to Dad's with Joey."

"How can we be sure?"

Loud rustling in the woods brought his head around. Kiley jumped to her feet, and lifted a limb the size of a club over her head, and Rob jumped to his feet beside her.

Dax Russell emerged from the foliage, stopped in his tracks and held up both hands. "Easy, easy, I'm not here to fight." His gaze was zipping from Rob's face to Kiley's makeshift weapon. "You wouldn't really hit me with that, would you?"

"Shhhhheeze," she breathed, and dropped the limb onto the

ground. "You scared the life outta me. What are you doing out here, Dax?"

"Same thing you are, I imagine." He nodded at Rob. "I...I owe you an apology."

"I owe you one back." Rob extended a hand.

Dax took it and shook. Then he looked at Kiley again. "You lied to me. You don't know how bad I suffered, thinking she was really dead."

"You only thought it for a couple of days, Dax. I thought it for almost two months. I thought she died in that fire. She played me, same as she played you."

"But you knew it was a lie when I showed you that picture."

She lowered her eyes. "Yeah, I was pretty sure this was some kind of scam when you told me the timing. But I wasn't convinced until I went home and found her waiting for me in my house."

"Kiley was going to find you and tell you the truth, Dax. I can vouch for that," Rob said.

Dax nodded, accepting that.

"How did you find us?" Kiley asked.

He lowered his eyes guiltily. "I've been watching your house. I figured she'd show up sooner or later, if she was alive. When she did, I followed her back to that saloon where she's been staying." Kiley sent a nervous glance Rob's way. He shook his head while staring at the ground. "I just knew she couldn't be dead. God, I was so glad to see her—but pissed off, too."

"I know the feeling," Kiley said. "So you followed her back here and then what?"

"I had to think. And drink. Did more drinking than thinking. Then I sobered up and came back here."

"To do what?" she asked.

"Talk to her. Give her a chance to give the money back before I call the cops and tell them what she did."

Rob saw her knee-jerk reaction to the notion of him calling

the cops. She glanced down at the ground where she'd dropped her limb-club, then back at Dax again.

She sighed, sent Rob a look that seemed to say *being the good guy is hard*, then lifted her chin, looked Dax in the eye. "She'll tell you she has the money stashed somewhere, and that she has to go get it. Then she'll skip town and you'll never see her or the money again."

"Besides," Rob added, "If you tell them what she did, you'll have to tell them what you did, won't you? You really want that to come out?"

He shot Rob an angry look, then Kiley an accusing one.

She shrugged. "I tell him pretty much everything." It wasn't entirely true, but she was getting there.

"Lucky guy," Dax said. Then he sighed. "So what were *you* planning to do?" he asked.

"I was just waiting for her to leave. Then I was gonna break into her room to look for the money she took from you."

He lifted his brows high. "Really?"

"Yeah. Really. I'm a respectable woman. That's how we roll." She glanced at Rob, and he gave her an encouraging nod. It wasn't her only reason for breaking in, but Dax didn't need to know that.

"And then what?" Dax asked.

"What do you mean, and then what?"

"If you found the money," he said. "Then what?"

"Then I'd give it back to you and tell you she was alive after all."

But only, Rob thought, after she'd given Kendra time to get out of town. She was determined to protect her sister. He'd probably do the same for either of his brothers.

Dax sat down on the log. "Maybe I fell for the wrong sister."

Rob stepped right up to Kiley, put his arm around her and said, "You picked the only sister that's available."

As he said it, Kiley looked at him wide eyed, but then Dax

sucked in a breath, and they both followed his gaze. Kendra had appeared, walking out from behind the saloon, talking on her cell and heading for her car.

"Just so you both know, there hasn't always been much of a difference," Kiley said. Her sister's car pulled onto the street and headed toward town.

Kiley looked at Rob, who gave a nod and said, "Let's go."

"This requires finesse, Rob. I need to go in alone. But I could use a couple of lookouts."

"I can do that," Dax said.

Rob shook his head. "I can't. I don't want you going in there without me, Kiley."

"It's your family's saloon, and there's no one there."

"There are other boarders in the other rooms."

"Who are probably out for the day since there's not a vehicle left in the driveway. And even if they aren't, if they see me, they'll think I'm her. Twins, remember?"

"Yeah. I remember." He sighed heavily. "It's Room One, my old room."

"I won't be long. Text me if anyone comes near the place, okay?"

"Will do." He held her eyes.

She leaned up and kissed him on the mouth. "Thanks for backing me up, Rob." She glanced at Dax. "You two play nice. You can talk horses or something."

Then she headed down onto the road, ran across it to The Long Branch, and hurried around to the back.

Rob sighed and returned to his seat on the log. "So what do you know about horses?" he asked.

"Everything," Dax replied.

~

The back door of The Long Branch Saloon, where she'd met Rob for the very first time, and taken, unknowingly, her first wobbling steps on the road to redemption, was unlocked. Kiley hurried inside, through the spotless kitchen and the barroom. Her footsteps echoed a little, and she tried to walk more quietly, but the place was empty. She didn't feel a hint of anyone else around.

Heading up the stairs and through the hall, Kiley stopped at the door to Room 1, which used to be Rob's, and pulled her little pouch of tools out of her bag. It took about eight seconds, near as she could figure, to pick the lock. Simple. She made a mental note to suggest new locks on the guest rooms. Then she turned the knob and opened the door.

And there he was, sitting in a comfy-looking chair, just as handsome as he'd always been, smiling at her in a way that could charm the diamonds off a queen. It felt like all the air just rushed out of her lungs, and she couldn't seem to get it back.

"Eight point two seconds," her father said with a look at his watch. "That's good. You've been practicing." He got to his feet and opened his arms. "Hello, baby."

And for the life of her, Kiley couldn't stop herself from running into them. She hugged him hard and choked on her tears, and moved her mouth to say something, but no sound came out.

"I missed you, little girl," he said. "You stopped coming to visit. Broke your old man's heart."

"I know." She sniffled, swallowed, cleared her throat. "I'm sorry, Dad. I tried to explain—"

"That's okay. It's all okay. I got your letter. Didn't believe it, but your sister says it's true. You're trying to go straight. Lead a normal life."

She sniffed again, stepped back a little. "Not just trying. I'm doing it."

He nodded, but she didn't think he believed her. His pale

blue eyes were searching, and his dimples not as deep as when his joy was genuine. "And you bought back the old place."

She nodded. "Half of it."

"Right, right. Kendra said you conned—sorry—*partnered* with one of the McIntyre boys for the other half."

"Yes."

"And where'd you get your half of the cash, little girl?" There was something in his tone. Something she knew and hated. Calculation. Intent.

She took three steps backward, shocked. He wasn't looking at her like a daughter he loved. He was looking at her like a threat he intended to eradicate. "I borrowed it. And I'll pay it back."

"You borrowed it." He shrugged one shoulder. "From a whole lot of donors in a scam I'd have been proud to call my own." He pulled a sheet of paper from his pocket, waved it under her nose. It was a printout of the web page she'd set up to collect donations for her imaginary dog's imaginary surgery. It even had a video of a poor little chihuahua with no back legs, dragging himself around. "I'm not criticizing," her father went on. "Hell, I'm impressed. But um, it doesn't really seem right now, does it? You get to run your game, get what you need, then get all high and mighty and decide to throw a wrench into your sister's plans. That *is* why you're here, isn't it? To find the money that lovesick hulk gave her, and give it back to him?"

As he spoke, he picked up a set of binoculars from the windowsill and looked through them out the window that faced the street. "Dax Russell chose to steal from his father's company for the sake of a pretty girl. He has no one to blame but himself."

"He was in love with her."

"And that makes what he did more legal?" He shook his head. "I'm real sorry to step into your happy little life of respectability, Kiley, but let me just explain to you how this is gonna happen."

"How what is gonna happen?" she asked. And her heart fluttered like a trapped bird. Her father and her sister were better at this game than she was. They always had been.

He lowered the binoculars and smiled at her. That fake smile he used to woo money out of rich ladies' purses. "How *you*, little girl, are gonna help keep the dogs off your sister me, so we can wrap up our work here, be on our way and out of your life. And how if you don't…well, I'm gonna have to tell that boyfriend of yours everything you did to get what you got. You cross me, I might just tell some eager DA somewhere as well. You understand?"

But she was going to tell him anyway.

Wasn't she?

"Well?"

She lowered her head, shaking it slowly. "What's the game? What are you up to here? Not Joey McIntyre. I can't let you—"

"He's a distraction, maybe some petty cash. No, we've got bigger irons in the fire, but you don't need to know what they are."

"Yes I do. What else have you two been up to in Big Falls?"

He just smiled. "We haven't been in Big Falls. We've been holing up in Tucker Lake. We only showed up here to make sure you weren't about to ruin all our plans. Once you met with Dax Russell, we knew the jig was up."

"Yeah. Cause I found out my sister was alive and letting me think she was dead. When did you even get out of prison?"

"Two months ago. They forwarded your letter."

"You…" She blinked, doing mental math. "You were out before Kendra faked her death?" He said nothing. "You knew. You knew the whole time. Hell, you probably helped her. And you, both of you, just let me believe she was dead."

"Only for a few weeks, honey."

"Almost two months!"

"It was for the greater good. We both knew you'd come running back to Big Falls once you got the news. We knew we'd catch up with you here. What we didn't anticipate was you deluding yourself into thinking you could change into someone you're not."

"I'm not deluding myself."

"Yes, you are, Kiley. You're a crook. You were born a crook, you were raised by crooks, and you'll die a crook. The quicker you accept that, the happier you'll be. So you just go on home now and mull that over. And tomorrow night, you're gonna invite your sister and me, and that handsome young billionaire boy Joey, to dinner at your place so your sister can make some more headway charming him into keeping quiet about her being here. Play up the whole family angle. The McIntyres seem to like that sort of thing. Now, go run along like a good girl. Plan your menu or whatever you *normal* people do."

Kiley blinked at her father, not believing the coldness in his eyes, in his tone. "Did you ever love me at all?" she asked.

"What, you do melodrama now, too?"

She just turned away and walked out of the room, down the stairs and out the front door. Then she headed across the street to where Rob was still waiting.

He smiled at her approach and got up onto his feet, but his smile died the closer she got. "What happened?"

Dax said, "You didn't find the money, did you?"

"No, Dax. I didn't."

He nodded. "Hell. I'm gonna have to report all of this and face the music, then." A deep nasal inhale, then, "I guess I have it coming."

"No you don't. This is my sister's fault, not yours. You don't deserve this." She looked at Rob, pleading.

He clapped Dax on the shoulder. "Don't turn yourself in. Look if it comes down to it, I can float you a loan to cover the shortage."

"You'd do that for me?" Dax asked. He almost looked like he was afraid he was being conned again.

"I'd do it for her," he said with a look at Kiley. Then he turned back to Dax. "Where you staying?"

"The Waterfront Hotel in Tucker Lake."

Rob nodded. "I've got your number," he said. "I'll call you when I get everything arranged."

Dax pressed his lips tight, nodded once, grabbed Rob's hand and shook hard. "I'll pay back every dime. And I'll still owe you one."

"I'll take it in free advice, once the mares arrive."

Dax clapped him on the shoulder, gave Kiley a nod, and went traipsing up the hill into the woods. He seemed to know where he was going.

"You didn't have to do that," Kiley said.

He shrugged. "You were right, Dax is a decent guy. When you told me he managed a race track, I thought you meant NASCAR or something. Not horses."

"He hates his job, but loves the animals. Maybe you can steal him at some point."

"Maybe I can." Rob put an arm around her shoulders and said, "You uh...you were gone a long time, in there."

She nodded.

"I could see through the curtain." He nodded toward the second-story window. "Who's the guy?"

Lifting her head, she met his eyes. His kind, caring, worried eyes, so different from the calculating, cool, lying eyes of her dad. "My father. He um...he's fresh out of prison," she said softly. "Been there for the last ten years."

"For...?"

"Same kind of thing Kendra did to Dax. Only on a much bigger scale, and it turned out a helluva lot worse. He seduced a married woman, took her money and then left her. Her husband found out, shot her and then himself."

"Holy God."

"Dad went up for manslaughter."

"I'm stunned he's already out," Rob said.

Kiley shrugged. "He's a con man. Best one I ever met," she said. "Taught Kendra and me everything we know. And now he's here, and he's up to something, and I don't know what, and I can't stop him and—"

"He taught you everything *he* knew," Rob said.

"What?" She didn't see the difference.

"He taught you everything he knew," Rob said. "Then he went to prison when you were, what, twelve?"

She nodded.

"While he was away, Kendra was out there honing her craft on unsuspecting guys like Dax. Maybe...you were, too?"

"Trying to. Yeah. I'm not proud of it."

He shrugged. "So that means by now you probably know more than he does. And if that's the case, then you can figure out what he's doing, and you can stop him."

Kiley lifted her head slowly. "No one beats Jack Kellogg."

"Someone did, or he wouldn't have been in prison." He sighed, and squeezed her tighter, pulling her against him. "You're gonna get through this. I'm gonna help you."

# CHAPTER TWELVE

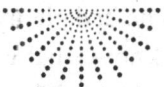

*W*hen they got back to the ranch, there was a battered pickup truck sitting in the driveway. A giant in bib overalls was looking at the piles of junk outside the barn.

He turned, nodded their way as they got out of the truck and approached him, then held out a long arm with a dinner plate sized hand at the end of it and said, "Erskine Rowe. Miz Vidalia sent me."

Rob shook hands with the man. "I've heard a lot about you from Vidalia," he said. "Good to put a face with the name."

He was an elderly gent with an eye for a treasure, who was, according to Vidalia, almost as rich as Bobby Joe. You'd never know it to see him. His well-worn bib overalls were about two inches too short for him. He wore a straw hat, and had a long face and a ready smile. "You've got some real finds here, son," he said.

"Oh yeah?"

Erskine nodded, looking around. There was the kind of sparkle in his eyes that Rob probably had when he talked about horses. "Oh, yeah. Some of the blacksmith equipment is true vintage, and in top condition. And that carriage over there—that's worth ten grand, easy."

Rob looked at Kiley with his brows raised. "That's gonna go a long way."

"You'll double that with the rest of these things."

"I can't believe this stuff has been here all this time, and we never even knew," Kiley said. "Dad was always trying to find ways to make a buck, and he had plenty right under his nose."

"Guess you just never know what you've got," Rob said.

"Two ways we can work this," Erskine said. "I can sell it on consignment, keep twenty percent. You'll make more money that way, but it'll take longer. Or I can give you twenty thousand for everything. Full disclosure, I could make more that way. Possibly as much as a third, but you'd have the funds right now."

Rob nodded and looked at Kiley. "What do you think?"

"I think if we had the money now, we could use it to get the ranch earning that much sooner."

"I agree. We'll take twenty-five for everything," Rob said.

Erskine narrowed his eyes and his face wrinkled like a baseball mitt. "I believe my offer was twenty."

"Well, that was your opening bid, yeah. And my counter is twenty-five. There are ten dealers I can think of within a thirty-mile radius. I can call around, see if any of them are willing to—"

"Twenty-five." The old man turned and shuffled back to his old, gray pickup truck. "I'll send the funds over with the boys when they bring the flatbed this evenin'." Then he got into his truck and it spit and sputtered to life, then rumbled away.

Kiley looked at Rob, and her eyes sparkled like diamonds. And right out of the blue, she slung her arms around his neck and hugged him hard. "I can't believe it!"

He grinned and picked her right up off her feet, spun her in a circle while she laughed out loud, and then set her down again. And as she stared up into his eyes, her smile died slow and her eyes went smoky. He felt that uncanny pull and leaned down, wrapped her closer, and kissed the living daylights out of her.

And she kissed back. Their mouths parted, tongues wrestled, bodies pressed tighter. His heart kicked into overdrive, and his blood got so hot it burned from the inside.

And then suddenly, she pulled away.

He blinked, disappointed right to his toes.

She said, "I'm sorry. I just...I have some...things."

"I know you do. I've pretty much decided it doesn't matter."

"I'm gonna work them out. I'm close."

"And you're gonna tell me."

She bit her lip, lowered her eyes.

"You said you were gonna tell me."

Nodding hard, she said, "I know. I want to. I'm just..."

"You just still don't trust me enough," he finished for her. "Not even after today."

She didn't answer, and he sensed that was because she was trying not to lie to him. "I... we need to have my father and my sister over for dinner tomorrow night, along with your brother Joey, if that's okay with you."

"You said I shouldn't trust your sister around my family, Kiley."

"And you said your family could spot a pretty con a mile away."

He nodded.

She lifted her chin and met his eyes. "I am giving you my word, right now, that I won't let her hurt your family. You have to believe me."

He took a long, slow breath. "Even though you've been lying from the start, right, Kiley?"

She swallowed hard, he saw her throat move.

He took a big breath. "I could choose to risk trusting you enough to partner with you on this place, even enough to share the house with you, because it was my risk to take. No one was gonna get hurt but me, if I was wrong."

"You're not wrong."

"But now you're asking me to put my family at risk. Joey falls in love if a girl looks at him too long. I've been brought to my knees by a woman who lied. I can't watch him go through that."

She lowered her head, nodded slow. He sighed, too. "If you'd just tell me, just trust me enough to tell me...."

She nodded. "I need a shower," she said. "It's been a long day."

She headed for the house, head hanging low, no bounce in her step at all. Dammit, she was gonna drive him to drink. He slapped his hat against his jeans, and hurried to catch up to her. "It's your house too, Kiley. I don't have any right to tell you who you can or can't invite to dinner."

She stopped walking, didn't look at him, just stopped, head still down. "So...tomorrow night?"

"Tomorrow night."

She looked up at him, smiled, but it didn't reach her eyes. They were full of worry and fear and he didn't even know what else.

"Thank you, Rob. I promise, this is all gonna be over soon."

He didn't like the little shiver of trepidation that ran up his spine when she said that, but he nodded all the same, and she kissed his mouth fast, then turned and hurried into the house.

Stress, worry, fear of what her family was doing in Big Falls, not to mention Kendra playing with Joey's feelings, were eating away at Kiley from the inside. And on top of it all, the fear of what they'd do to her entire life if she tried to stop them. She'd been racking her brain all night to figure a way out of all of this, but she hadn't come up with a thing.

"Mail call," Rob said when he came inside. He'd been out helping Erskine's guys load all the stuff from the barns onto a flatbed truck.

He dropped a pile of mail on the kitchen counter, but Kiley didn't look at it. She was too busy looking at him. His T-shirt was tight, so his chest was kind of strutting its stuff. And then she noticed his biceps, and the hairs on his forearms, and those strong, hands of his, and everything she'd been worrying about evaporated from her mind.

"Kiley?"

"What?" She blinked, jerked her eyes up to meet his and said, "Sorry. I'm just...distracted."

He moved closer to her, pressed his hands to her shoulders, and then ran them up and down her outer arms. "Family stuff is hard. And I know yours is a little messed up right now. Mine was too, until we all came out here and Vidalia adopted a passel of grown men into her brood. Family first, that's the Brand motto. And it's become the McIntyre's too." He smiled crookedly. "I guess you could call it our step-motto."

She couldn't help but laugh.

"I gotta say, I like it better than my dad's former motto."

"And what was that?" Kiley asked.

"'If there's not a profit to be made, drop it and move on.'" His expression turned serious as he said it, and she knew he wasn't teasing any more. "Your family have a motto, Kiley?"

"Not officially," she thought for a moment. "But my father used to say about a hundred times a day, 'if you're dumb enough to be taken, you deserve it.'"

"That's harsh," he said.

She smiled up at him, trying to get back to the lightness of the earlier conversation. "Yeah. I like the Brand family motto better."

"So do I." He kissed her on the forehead, and said, "Relax. Tonight will go fine, I promise. And Joey said he'd stop at the diner on the way out, pick up the giant take-out order I just placed."

"Oh, I wish you hadn't asked him to do that. Guests shouldn't have to being their own food. I was gonna heat up Maya's frozen lasagna."

"He offered, and he doesn't mind." He tugged his T-shirt away from his skin and wrinkled his nose. "I need to hit the shower. There's a Big Falls' Big Future flyer in that pile of mail. All the local landowners have made donations, and we're landowners now. You should look it over and we'll talk about it later."

"Okay."

He headed through the house and up the stairs, and Kiley watched him go and wondered what was happening to her head. She was literally pining for the guy. And she wondered how much longer he was going to want to take things slowly. She was ready to kick things up a notch.

But she knew she was the one keeping barriers between them. Her secrets were what stood in the way. She had to break those walls down, open up to him, tell him the truth.

But she had to deal with her dad and sister first. She didn't want to see either of them in prison. Especially not her sister.

Sighing, she wandered to the counter and picked up the stack of mail, flipping through it. She stopped on the big yellow envelope with the sunshine logo address label on the front that read Big Falls' Big Future.

She opened the envelope, pulled out the paperwork inside. A cover letter, and a slick trifold brochure that showed reservoirs in other towns. There were images of lush green parks linings their shores, designated swimming areas, playgrounds filled with happy children, kayakers, canoeists, fishermen and blue, blue water with diamond ripples glittering in the sun.

She started reading the text and then she stopped and her heart seemed to freeze into a chunk of ice in her chest. "Oh my God," she whispered. "Oh. My. *God.*"

"What? What is it?"

She spun around, clutching the flyer to her chest and blinking at Rob. He'd come back downstairs for something. He wasn't wearing a shirt, just jeans. She was almost too stunned by the revelation to notice. "I...I..."

Frowning, he came closer, took the flyer from her, looked at it, then at her again. "Kiley? Jeeze, you're white as a sheet. Sit down."

She sank into a kitchen chair. He pulled out a second one, turned it backwards and straddled it, facing her. "Now tell me what's wrong."

She blinked, met his eyes, and said, "I don't have a choice. I have to."

She lowered her head, too ashamed to look him in the eye. "My father's behind Big Falls, Big Future."

He frowned, clearly not getting it. "What do you mean, he's behind it?"

"I mean it's a scam. All that money the locals have been raising and donating. He's just going to take it and leave town."

He took the flyer again, looked at it as if he could see the truth there. "How do you know?" he asked.

Closing her eyes, she said, "Because I wrote it."

Rob took it upon himself to call Kendra on her sister's phone, and postpone their dinner. Then he called the diner in time to cancel his takeout order, popped that frozen lasagna into the oven, and scoured the cabinets for alcohol. He was fairly certain there had been a few bottles of something among all the gifts and supplies his family had brought over. And Lord knew he was going to need it. His little con-artist was about to come clean.

Whiskey. It would do. He filled two glasses with ice, poured the whiskey over, then added Coke and carried the glasses into the living room.

Kiley was sitting on the sofa. He handed her a glass and sat down beside her. She sipped, swallowed, then sipped again. "We went into foster care after Dad went to prison. They put us in separate homes. It tore me up. Her, too, I think."

"I'm sorry."

"We tried to stay in touch, but it wasn't easy. When we turned eighteen they just cut us loose. But at least we had each other."

"What did you do?" he asked, watching her face, trying to imagine being eighteen with no home, no job and no money and just being expected to figure it out. He needed to remember to thank his parents for the childhood he'd had.

"We did the only thing we knew how to do. Ran a game. I was good with words, so I put the flyer together. Fundraiser to create a dog park in a small neighborhood. PO Box address to send donations. Kendra got a job at a print shop, just long enough to run them off. We pulled in five grand."

"Wow."

"I felt terrible about it. I knew I couldn't keep living that way." She lowered her head, seemed to be looking inside herself. "It just galvanized Kendra. She was so high on pulling it off, she starting coming up with bigger, better cons. She was furious when I told her I wasn't interested. We split the money, I went my way, she went hers."

"Okay. What did you do then?"

"I got an apartment upstate, went through a dozen jobs, waitress, convenience store clerk, bartender, fast-food worker. From time to time I'd have to run a game to pay the rent.

Nothing elaborate. Sob story to a co-worker, or a date. That kind of thing."

Again, he just nodded and listened.

"And then I got the news that my sister had died. They sent me her ashes. And I just…"

"Fell apart," he said. He moved closer, put an arm around her shoulders.

"I wanted to come home, started looking for news about Big Falls online. Found out the place was going to be auctioned."

He was half afraid to hear the rest, but he braced himself for it, told himself it wouldn't be that bad.

"I knew I had to come home. I couldn't bear to see my home auctioned to strangers. I thought—I thought just one con, a big one, and it would be my last one ever."

Rob closed his eyes.

"I put up a website with a video of a chihuahua who'd lost his hind legs. Spun a big sob story about my best friend needing expensive prosthetics, and asked for donations. It went viral. In three weeks, I had half of what I needed to buy back the place."

He felt like he'd been hit in the chest with wrecking ball. The breath just left his lungs. And he tipped his head back, stared at the ceiling. "You stole the money to buy the ranch."

"I never considered it stealing."

"What you considered it doesn't change what it was, Kiley. It was stealing. You stole…half a million dollars." Saying it out loud made it seem even worse, not that much probably could. "My God, do you know what kind of time you'd do for that?"

She closed her eyes. "I kept the email addresses of every person who donated. I'm going to pay them all back."

"How?"

"I don't know."

He was angry. Really angry. He got up and paced the room. This couldn't be happening. My God, she wasn't just a petty con, she was a major criminal. And there was no way this wouldn't come out, no way she wouldn't end up in prison.

God, he didn't want her to end up behind bars.

He got an idea, and said, "What if I—?"

"No." She stood up, too. "You're not loaning me the money to pay them all back. I have to do this myself."

He stared into her eyes, saw her resolve there, believed she meant what she said. But hell, she'd stolen a half million dollars. "But Kiley, how?"

"I'll figure it out. But in the meantime, I've got a bigger problem to deal with. That flyer," she said, with a look at it lying on the counter. "It's got entire paragraphs lifted from the dog park scam my sister and I ran before we split up. Some of the graphics are even the same. She just changed it enough to apply to a reservoir instead of a dog park. My father and my sister are about to rob our friends and neighbors and your family. Last time I saw one of those Big Falls' Big Future signs, the red in the thermometer was up to three-hundred and fifty thousand."

He nodded. "You're right. We have to stop them. Maybe it's time to call Jimmy."

"*I* have to stop them. Not *we*. And I'm not bringing the police into this."

"Jimmy's family."

She shook her head. "My father knows about my chihuahua scam, Rob. He'll turn me in if he finds out I'm trying to do anything to stop him."

He walked up to her, took her by the shoulders. "Listen to me, okay? This is a pivotal moment for us. Are you getting that?"

She lowered her head. "Pivotal. Like it's not already over? Like you're going to want anything to do with me after this? You, the guy who vowed not to tell a lie if you could help it? You're still going to want anything to do with me now that you know what I've done?"

He held her eyes for a long moment, then lowered his head.

"That's why I couldn't tell you, Rob. I knew—"

"No you didn't. You can't possibly know what's going on in my head, so don't think you do. The only thing I'm sure about is that we can't let your father and your sister scam this entire town and get away with it."

"I don't plan to."

"He's screwing with my family, Kiley. So you've got two choices here."

"Oh, hell," she said, turning away and pushing a hand through her hair.

"You either let me help you stop him, or I call Jimmy and turn them in."

"You do, and I go down with them."

"You don't make this right, you probably deserve to." He sighed heavily. "But I'll give you a head start to get out of town." He picked up the flyer, looked at it, shook his head in disgust and threw it on the counter. "That's the best offer you're gonna get from me. Take it or leave it."

She felt like screaming. Fighting. Crumbling on the floor and crying. "That's no choice at all, Rob. I guess I'll take it."

# CHAPTER THIRTEEN

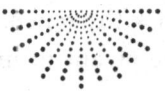

*S*omehow, he managed not to go off like a bomb, or curl into a corner like a boiled shrimp. Somehow, he managed to hold the broken pieces of himself into a semblance of the man he was for the next several hours. They stayed up late, talking and listening. But only about her father and sister. Not about them. Not about the bomb she'd just dropped on the fragile seedling of whatever had been growing between them. Not about anything important.

Just about little things, like saving the town.

"Keep your focus on the goal," he said, for about the tenth time. She kept sliding off onto side roads, like keeping her family out of jail. Then she'd gone through six permutations of an escape plan for them, and swilled a bottle of Algernon West with each one. He had to keep pulling her back on point. "Remember the goal? The goal is to get the town's money back."

"Right. And the *trick* is...." She tipped the longneck to her lips, then frowned and tipped it upside down, shaking it a little. Nothing came out.

"Go on, tell me. The trick is what?"

Her round blue eyes met his. "The trick is to make Dad think it was his idea to give it to us."

"Why would he want to give it to us?" he asked.

"Lots of reasons. Maybe I need a kidney," she said with a smile. And he knew that she knew that would never work. "Or maybe we have something he wants."

"You mean, the ranch?" he asked. His stomach twisted a little. He didn't want to risk the ranch. It was right then he realized how much this place meant to him. Already. "He wants it back?"

"No." She set the empty on the table, then leaned back on the sofa and put her bare feet up there beside it. "We have to make him want it. And there's only one thing my father wants. Money. So we make him want to buy back part of the ranch."

"Three hundred and fifty thousand dollars worth of it?" he asked.

She nodded once. "We can let on that we fought. You found out the truth about my past and you want no more to do with me." Her voice got thick, and she stopped, swallowed, and said, "Is there anymore beer?"

"We make him think one of us might be willing to sell our half bad enough to take a loss."

She nodded. "I'm not anywhere drunk enough."

"I need you to not get any drunker, though. We need to figure this out." He sat around the corner of the modular sofa from her, his feet up beside hers on the coffee table. "Kiley?"

"What?"

"How can we make your father want to buy into the ranch?"

She shrugged. "I don't know. We'd have to find gold in the river or strike oil or something."

He grinned. "Yeah, maybe there's a diamond mine out back or— Hey, we don't really need to strike oil or find gold. We just need him to believe we did."

She sat up on the sofa and picked up one of her empties,

tipped it up to look inside, and reached for another. "We can't jus' tell'm. It'd be transparent."

"Maybe we could help him find out by accident?"

"He has to find out by snooping. He's a turble snoop. Turrble. Rhymes with gerbil. Who knew?" She leaned her head back on the sofa, closed her eyes.

"Okay. Okay, I think I've got an idea. What if we—"

The sound of a wildebeest choking on a grizzly bear, interrupted his thought. Kiley's snore was so loud it startled her awake, and she sat up, blinking like she didn't know where she was. Then her eyes landed on him, and she relaxed, smiled.

She was a cute drunk.

He looked over at her, and thought he was kind of in over his head. "I wish I understood you."

"No point trying, Robby. There's a whole lot about me no one's ever gonna understand." Her words were sloshing into each other.

"How do you know unless you give someone a chance to try?"

She stared up at him for a long time, frowning so hard it made him grin. "I gave you a chance to try. How's it goin' so far?"

God, he had fallen hard for her. Harder than he knew. It wouldn't hurt this bad otherwise.

He held out his hands. "Help you to bed?"

"You coming with me?" She pointed at him in six-gun position, clicked her tongue twice, and tried to wink. It seemed to be more things than she could manage at once, and the wink looked more like her face had melted on one side.

"Just wouldn't be honorable, ma'am. He fake-tipped a nonexistent hat.

"You're a true cowboy, aren't you, Robby McIntyre?"

"I try to be." He scooped her right up off the sofa. She locked her arms around his neck, pulling herself up so she could nuzzle his throat as he carried her up the stairs. It tickled when she spoke against his neck. "I really like you."

"I like you, too." His voice was raspy as whiskers on silk. God, she got to him.

She leaned up and kissed his chin. "I like your family, too."

He'd made it to the top of the stairs, and turned to head down the hall to her bedroom. The whole time a voice inside his head was yelling, *This is not a good idea!* He turned the knob and opened the door, saw her unmade bed, and clothes scattered around the floor. "Not a neat thing, are you?"

"I like it messy." Then she laughed very deeply and softly. "I don't even know what that means, but it sounded sexy. Didn't it?" She threaded her fingers up over his nape and into his hair, pulling his head down and lifting her own up.

She brushed his lips with hers.

Robby's soul caught fire, and he almost lost it. In the nick of time, he dropped her onto the bed out of sheer desperation, and the breath huffed out of her when she landed.

She looked up at him, eyes as round and wounded as a whipped pup's. "I don't think I can take it if you hate me."

"Hasn't been a man born who could hate you, Kiley Kellogg."

He went back through the door and closed it behind him. And then he wiped the sweat from his forehead onto his sleeve, and headed for the shower

# CHAPTER FOURTEEN

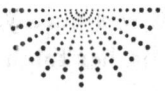

The gentle tap on Kiley's bedroom door made her feel as if her head had been tossed into a dryer set to tumble. With a bucketful of rocks. *Sharp* rocks. She said, "Knock again and die," but the sound that emerged was a muffled "Nogundee."

The door opened, the familiar squeak of the hinge like nails on a chalkboard, and the soft step of sock-feet, like the approach of Godzilla.

Then the smell of something ambrosial filled her nostrils, soothing the steady thud in her head just a little.

She opened one eye. Male forearms, in rolled-back sleeves, big strong hands, one of them holding a plate with a giant, still-steaming, blueberry-oozing muffin. Butter melted from the top and spilled down the sides like the tears of her guardian angel. The other hand, just as tanned and sexy, held the elixir of the gods in a stoneware mug, steaming even more than the muffin was.

"You're not really human, are you?" she whispered, and it hurt her ears.

He handed her the coffee first, like he could read her need for it.

She scootched up higher onto her pillows, cupped the mug in her palms and brought it to her lips, sipping. Her brain cells opened like flowers in the morning sun. "Nirvana," she whispered.

She sipped again, and then opened her eyes enough to locate that muffin. Her stomach was queasy, but carbs might absorb the ick. She set the plate on her thighs, broke off a small piece and ate it, chewing slowly, savoring every taste.

"God, that's good." She broke off another piece. "Thanks. I don't deserve you."

He sat on the edge of her bed. "Kiley, listen. I don't play games. I don't hide anything. I'm straight-up honest. What you see is what I am. Nothing to puzzle out or uncover. You get that, right?"

She ate her second piece of muffin, then smacked her thumb and forefinger. "Are you about to ruin this incredible moment with serious talk?" she asked. "You are, aren't you?"

"'Fraid so."

"Wait." Holding up a forefinger, she ate another piece of the muffin, a bigger piece this time. Then she sipped the coffee, then sipped it again. One final sip and she leaned back against the headboard and nodded. "Okay, go ahead. No, wait." She grabbed another bite of the muffin, then said, "Mmkay." She washed it down with more coffee, then looked at him expectantly.

He didn't say anything.

She said, "I kind of thought we could talk about the...you know, the us stuff...after we send my family packing. Cause, if it doesn't work, the rest is kind of gonna be decided for us. I'll either be in Mexico or in jail."

He took a deep breath, tried to count to ten and only got to four. "Are you a part of your family's con?"

She blinked at him. "What do you mean?"

"Are you a part of it? Is this, all this," he waved an open palm in a half circle. "Is all of it part of some bigger game? Are you just—"

"Jeeze, Rob." She slid right out the other side of the bed, and put her bare feet on the floor. She'd pulled her blanket with her, but realized she didn't need it. She was still fully clothed. "I thought you trusted me. I thought you said you'd give me the benefit of the doubt. I thought—"

"I want to trust you, dammit. But you've been lying to me since you came here."

She marched across the room and faced him. "I haven't told you one thing that wasn't true since the day you asked me not to lie."

"But you haven't told the truth either. Still."

"About what?" she asked in a squeaky voice.

"God only knows. I feel like there must be a hundred things. But we could start with the ring." She frowned. "Your grandmother's ring? The one that went into the drain when I hit you with my truck?"

She closed her eyes. "I kind of...forgot about that."

"You forgot?"

"It didn't work. I didn't get you to give me any money. You bought half the ranch instead. Believe me, that was not my plan."

He rolled his eyes. "It was a lie. And things started up between us and you still didn't tell me."

She blinked at him. "I...I'm sorry." He lowered his head, and she closed the distance between them, put her hands on his shoulders. "No, I mean it. I'm sorry. Rob, I'm trying. I am. I'm afraid I'm just not very good at this."

He hadn't responded. Not in any way. Dejected, she dropped her hands to her sides. "Maybe I'm trying to be something I'm not."

"What, honest?"

"You really know how to ruin a great breakfast, you know that?" She sent a regretful look at the muffin, sitting on its plate atop her blanket on the bed. The coffee was still clutched in her hand. You couldn't have pried it away with a crowbar. "I'm gonna take a shower."

"Kiley, don't. Don't brush me off this way. We need to talk about this."

"No we don't. You've got to decide whether or not you can accept me for who I am. Not who I'm trying my ass off to become, but who I am, right now, right here."

"How the hell can I do that when you won't *show* me who you are?"

"I am showing you," she said. "I know it took me too long, but I'm showing you now. I opened up to you last night. And you backed away, just like I knew you would. Face it, Rob. You're too good for the likes of a Kellogg girl."

He put his hands on her outer arms and stared down into her face. "Then why am I falling in love with one?"

"Falling in love...?" The muffin and the coffee chose that moment to launch their escape attempt. She clapped a hand over her mouth, ducked beneath his right arm and ran for the bathroom.

Kiley leaned against the gate post at the end of the driveway. Tonight, she and Rob were having that dinner with her dad and Kendra, which they'd put off for two more nights. The dinner wasn't happening at the ranch, but rather at The Long Branch. She was more nervous than she'd ever been in her life. Her father was better than her. Her sister was phenomenal. And Kiley was the screw up, the one who hadn't inherited the family gift. And she was going to try to outcon the two best cons she knew.

She was terrified.

So she pushed it from her mind, because this morning was special.

Two posts stood tall on either side of the driveway, with a big sign suspended in between. The sign was a rectangle, but it had a fancy border burned into its face. And inside that border, deep gouges in the wood formed a western sort of font that spelled out HOLIDAY RANCH.

Rob's whole family had gone in on it, had it custom made as a ranch-warming gift, as they'd put it.

Rob stood across the driveway from her, leaning on the opposite post, watching the empty road as intently as she was. He was wearing a Stetson. He hardly ever wasn't these days.

They hadn't talked any more about their relationship. She didn't know if he regretted what he'd said to her or not. Or if he'd meant it in the past tense. He hadn't touched her again, hadn't kissed her. She was aching with longing.

The Stetson looked good on him. She kind of loved it on him.

"I think I'm as excited as you are," she said, just to say something that was honest.

"This is a dream come true for me," he said, dragging his eyes off the horizon to look her way.

She didn't think he could stop himself from smiling if he tried. For a second she glimpsed the little boy he must've been once, and her heart did some odd kind of flip-flop in her chest. She just wished his eyes weren't shadowed by the weight of the mess she'd brought crashing into his life. The poor guy.

"I'm glad I get to be a part of this," she said. "Whatever else happens."

His face turned serious. "I'm glad about that, too."

The rumble of a semi-truck reached her ears, and she swung

her head around. "Here they come!" She just barely restrained herself from bouncing up and down and clapping her hands like a little girl when the ice cream truck stops near her house.

Rob stood up straighter and pushed the hat back on his head. Then he shot across to her side of the driveway.

The truck rolled through, clearing their sign with two feet to spare, she noted with relief. They ran along beside the blue livestock trailer, trying to get glimpses through its portholes.

Big brown eyes with thick paintbrush lashes here, a pink, twitching nostril there. A flash of shaking mane.

The truck swung around past the corral, kicking up a dust cloud, and then began backing up to its gate. Rob ran ahead to open it.

A minute later the driver got out, went around to the back, opened the trailer door and vanished inside. Kiley was almost holding her breath when the first young mare, cream colored with a paler mane and tail, came light-stepping her way out of the trailer and into the paddock. She was followed by another, her coat deep red-brown, and then another. Kiley kept thinking that every horse that came out was the prettiest, until the next one emerged.

Rob went to close the gate as the driver folded up the ramp and closed the trailer doors once again.

Eight mares pranced around the corral, manes and tails wafting in the blissfully cool breeze. Rob had told her the proper names for their colors when he'd shown her their pictures online. The blue-gray one was a blue roan, the black and white, a piebald. There was a palomino, a chestnut and a beautiful dark bay. But the most impressive of all was the dominant white, who was living up to her name. Their hooves raised up a dust cloud around them.

"God, they're beautiful."

Rob nodded and rested his head on top of hers just for a second, watching the mares prance.

"Got some papers for you to sign," the driver said.

Rob went around to the front of the truck with the driver.

Kiley watched the mares dance as they began to settle down. Their movements slowed and they started exploring their surroundings.

She loved it here. This place, this moment, she loved it. She wanted this to be her life. And she was trying to do the right thing. It was probably as likely to fail as to succeed, but she was trying. She hoped Rob could see that. It had hurt when he'd asked if she was working with her family. But she knew she couldn't blame him for it. She was a crook. She'd told him she was a crook. She'd played him.

But she'd changed. She was doing the right thing now, the good thing. The thing Vidalia Brand-McIntyre or one of her daughters would do.

She wanted to be a good person. And dammit, once she'd decided that, real clearly in her mind—it had cut loose inside her like a west coast mudslide. She couldn't stop it. It was challenging, and it was exciting, and it felt good. Trying to be a good person, doing what felt like a good thing, it filled a dark cavern inside her with honey-gold light, revealing a cave made of diamonds.

It felt like salvation.

At least it had, right up until Rob had learned who she'd been before.

It was heartbreaking. He was pulling away from someone who didn't exist anymore. And in the process, letting go of someone who might just be wonderful.

Or, you know, doing ten to twelve in Folsom.

She heard the rig's door slam, and then it growled its intentions and rolled back the way it had come. Rob watched it go, then came back to the corral. "Let's see how they like their new stompin' grounds."

"They're gonna love it." His joy was contagious. She had

never been so glad to be right where she was. She stopped worrying about what was to come, just put everything out of her mind except this amazing moment. They walked together around the corral, to the fence line that ran from the back of the stable, through a rolling meadow with shade trees, a small woody lot, and plenty of grasses and wildflowers. The river snaked its way right through it.

Kiley followed Rob around to the back side of the corral, where it intersected the meadow, and he opened the gate.

The mares knew exactly what to do. The white mare went first, prancing like a ballerina into the meadow, then broke into a full-on gallop for about twenty yards. She stopped and stood, just looking. The others trotted into the meadow one by one. Some explored, some went down to the river, and one began eating immediately. "Look, look at her. The blue roan, she's so beautiful."

"She's one of my favorites."

"And just look at *her*," Kiley said, watching the white mare checking things out. And then she reared up and cut loose a loud whinny that drew immediate attention from the other seven.

"You get the feeling she's telling them who's gonna be in charge around here?" Kiley asked.

"No question in my mind. Reminds me of Vidalia." He glanced down at her. "And you."

"Me?" She shook her head. "No way, I don't want to be in charge of anybody."

"You know what you want, and you do whatever it takes to get it," he said.

She stared at him hard. "That used to be true. It's not true anymore." She took a deep breath, looked him right in the eye and told herself to let him see her.

He leaned on the corral fence. He only could've looked more the cliché if he'd been chewing on a piece of hay. "I knew there was no ring. I knew it right from the start," he said.

"You did?"

He nodded. "I don't know if anyone's ever told you this, but you're a terrible liar."

Tears welled up and she automatically blurted, "Dad considered it my biggest flaw."

"I'm glad you're a bad liar. People who are inherently honest usually are."

"They are?"

"Yeah."

"So if you knew, then why did you buy in with me?"

"I wanted the place anyway. Wanted to get it without dipping into my inheritance if I could, and you seemed like the perfect solution. Besides, I thought you were cute and sweet and kinda sexy, and I loved your ideas about Holiday Ranch." He took a deep breath. "I knew what I was getting into. Decided to take the risk. So...if you're feeling guilty about tricking me, don't."

"Why are you telling me now?" She hoped it wasn't the beginning of a long goodbye.

"Because we're going to fight about this later, in front of your family. I don't want you to start thinking anything I might say then is real."

"Oh. Okay."

"Have you told me everything now?" he asked. "Is there anything else you haven't—"

"Everything," she said.

"You sure? You never killed anybody?"

"No!"

"You ever put anyone in the hospital? Kidnap their babies? Abuse their children?"

"No! God, what do you think I—"

He turned them around and, pressing her back to the side of

the barn, stared hard into her eyes. "Have you, Kiley Kellogg, ever kicked a dog?"

"Have I...what?" Her heart was beating faster. The way he was looking at her, oh, God, and snugging his body right up against hers. She could hardly catch her breath.

"Kicked a dog," he repeated. "Or any innocent animal. I can't abide animal cruelty. That's a deal breaker right there."

"No," she whispered in a voice rubbed with sandpaper. "Never."

"Good." He kissed her then. She didn't think he was gonna stop, either. She hoped not. She'd had enough of feeling cold and alone and longing for him to touch her again.

She was drunk right then. On him, on the taste of him, the scent of him, the intoxicating velvety brush of his lips over hers. She'd been so sure she'd lost him.

He kept on kissing her as he walked her off the barn wall and sideways, through its door. They stepped into cool darkness, the smell of oats with molasses, and hay, and new lumber. Still kissing, they fell into a pile of fresh hay, stacked loose in an alcove. It prickled her arms and her legs, but he'd grabbed a brand new horse blanket from a rack on the way past, and he spread it beneath them and moved her onto it.

The kissing went on. Not just her lips, no. He dropped kisses like a strand of pearls along her jawline, and into the hollow beneath her ear, sending shivers all the way to her toes, unbuttoning her shirt while he was at it. She realized it and tried to decide whether she was supposed to be unbuttoning his, but thinking was way beyond her scope just then. His lips trailed down one side of her neck, and curved around into the ultra-sensitive well at the front of her throat. She thought her body was going to melt into a puddle of pleasure.

Her blouse was gone. Bra, too, a second later. And then he was kissing her breasts and she stopped wondering anything, except how she could feel this much pleasure and not die from it.

And then she stopped thinking even that, because they were all wrapped up in each other, naked skin to naked skin, the most delicious friction there was.

It was two hours before another thought was able to gel inside her brain. And that, just a vague awareness, really, that what she felt for Rob was bigger than anything she'd ever felt in her life. Bigger than she knew she was capable of feeling. It was massive, infinite, all encompassing. It was...

Oh my God, was it love? Was this what love felt like? Could that be what this was?

What if she loved him?

# CHAPTER FIFTEEN

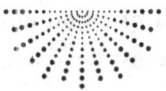

$\mathcal{R}$ ob spent the afternoon getting the stalls ready for the mares. Kiley had come out to join him. He was trying to keep things light between them, but it weighed on him heavily that their plan was going down tonight and might not work.

He didn't want to see her arrested for her crimes, not when she was trying so hard to change. And he didn't want to see her family steal from Big Falls. Partly because he loved the place and everyone in it. But mostly because he didn't think Kiley would ever forgive herself.

He didn't know anything for sure beyond that.

"God, it smells good in here," she said.

She looked right at home in a stable. It was that strawberry blond, sun-kissed, country-girl look, he supposed. "It's the grain." Rob inhaled. Every breath smelled like molasses. "I put a little bit in each stall. I want them to love it here."

"I'm pretty sure they already do."

"I was just getting ready to bring 'em in for the night. Want to help?"

"You think I came out here to do my nails?"

He smiled and nodded. "Close the front door. Jeeze, were you brought up in a barn?"

"Pretty much this very barn," she replied. "We were forbidden to come out here, but we did anyway. The hay loft wasn't full of junk like the rest of the place. We'd swing from the rafters, as a matter of fact." She looked up through the open trapdoor into the barn's second level as she said it. "We'd jump off the top of a mountain of baled hay up there. The old-fashioned rectangle-shaped bales. We'd use them like giant bricks to build a castle."

"You and Kendra?"

Her smile wavered a little. Dammit, what a dumb thing to say. He knew there was tension between her and her sister. Hurt, betrayal. He couldn't imagine one of her brothers doing to him what Kendra had done to Kiley. Twins were supposed to be tighter than other siblings, weren't they?

Quick, he thought, new subject. "I um...I want the mares to come when I call them, but I've gotta show 'em what's waiting when they get here."

"A girl needs a reason," she said, and gave him the once over. His ego grew a size and a half.

He led the way to the small tack room, then dipped into his feed bin and scooped a little grain into each of two pails. "Come on," he said, handing her one of them. "Follow my lead."

He opened the barn's back door, and they stepped directly into the meadow where the mares stopped munching on clover blossoms to look up at them, almost as one unit.

"I figure if we let 'em smell what we've got in these buckets, they'll follow us anywh—"

"Uh, yeah, totally unnecessary," Kiley interrupted.

The white mare came trotting right toward them, shaking her mane and blowing. She was high-stepping like a Rockette, and he thought he got the message. *I'm the boss, not you. Now gimme that grain.*

188

She stopped right in front of him, head down, nostrils flaring as she caught the scent of molasses and oats. He held the bucket just out of reach as she went for it.

The other seven had already gathered around to see what was going on and whether they could get themselves a taste of what smelled so good. Kiley backed into the barn first, holding her bucket out and staying ahead of them. The stalls were all open, and each one already had grain waiting inside, along with soft straw bedding and fresh clear water.

"Which stall for which horse?" Kiley asked, whispering like she didn't want to startle the mares.

"Let's let them decide." He went all the way to the front of the barn, taking her bucket from her on the way, and set them in the tack room and closed its door.

The mares didn't follow at first. The white one just stood in the doorway, taking them in. She could smell the grain, though. And she wanted it. Then finally, she came in, hoofs clacking sharp on the clean concrete floor. She poked her head into one stall, then backed out and walked directly to the one dead center, right hand side. She went right into it and buried her nose in her grain. The others came in and picked stalls seemingly at random. He and Kiley closed the stall doors as the horses went inside.

"Have you thought about names for them?"

He nodded. "The Blue Roan is the prettiest. And she's sly and clever. She was nuzzling the door earlier when I first came out. I think she smelled the grain and thought it was in here, unsupervised. I was gonna call her Kiley, but that could get confusing. What's your middle name?"

She was blinking like she had something in her eyes. "Louise."

"Okay. She's Louise. Which means the dun has to be Thelma. They seem to be best friends."

He was joking, but she wasn't laughing. She was standing in

front of the stall, looking in at Louise to avoid his eyes. It got to her, him naming that magnificent animal after her.

"What about the white?" she asked.

"Lady Vee." He said it with a firm nod. "She's the boss of the entire herd. Definitely gotta be Lady Vee."

"For Vidalia. That's perfect."

"So are you ready for this dinner?"

"Still gotta change clothes."

"Mentally, I meant. Emotionally. It's gonna be...intense."

"I'm trying to focus on The Long Branch's amazing cook."

"Chef. He'd be offended to be called a cook."

Two hours later, they were being shown to a table set for five as if they were guests in The Long Branch's fancy dining room. The decor was Old West as interpreted by the TV show *Gunsmoke.* There were red velvet drapes with gold rope tie-backs, marking the transition from barroom to dining room. The Miss Kitty lookalike was not played by Vidalia tonight, but often was, and Kiley was dying to see her in the role. She showed them to their table, which was on the opposite side of the room from the player piano. The bartender, Rob's older brother Jason, stood behind the bar in a white shirt with thin black suspenders and a bolo tie. He nodded as they'd walked in, but other than that, was giving them space.

"I keep forgetting how amazing this place is," Kiley said.

"I do, too. It's different being here as a guest instead of an owner."

"Yeah. That must be weird."

A young waitress dressed in a tamed-down version of saloon-girl attire, came to take their orders. She was new, and it struck Rob that he'd really been letting his brothers down in the running of the saloon. He was a full shareholder and wasn't doing his part. He was going to have to talk to them about that.

"Can I get you something to drink while you wait for your companions to arrive?"

"I'll take a beer," Kiley said. "One of those from that local microbrewery with the funny name. You know, Rob, the ones we had at the house—" She stopped there, bit her lip and then said, "You know what? I'll just have a sweet tea."

She was remembering how sick she'd been on that beer a few days ago. He saw the thought flit through her eyes almost as clearly as if it was flitting through his own head.

"Same for me," he said, and the waitress went away.

Kiley smiled at him, was about to say something, and then looked across the room, and said, "Shoot, here they come." Her smile died, her eyes turned cold, and she turned to watch her father and sister coming down the stairs and into the dining room.

Her dad was a handsome man who turned women's heads everywhere he went. His hair was still like dark honey, his eyes, still Newman blue. He came down the curving staircase slowly, his gaze sweeping everyone in the room. "The guys have been referring to them as Jack and Kendra Jones," Rob said. "I don't remember if you picked up on the alias."

"It's an old standby," Kiley muttered. "Here comes Joey. It's on. How's my resting bitch face?"

He glanced at her. She looked good and pissed. And yet, still beautiful. "Pretty convincing."

Then he rose as Joey, Kendra and Jack arrived at the table. He clapped his brother on the shoulder, and extended a hand to Kiley's dad. "It's good to meet you, Jack. I'm sorry it took so long." This with an irritated glance at Kiley.

She rolled her eyes and reached for her water glass.

Her sister frowned her way, but quickly readjusted and

beamed her bright, phony smile at Rob. "Nice to see you again," she said.

He nodded hello, and Joey pulled out a chair for Kendra, then took the one beside her. Jack sat down on her other side, taking the seat between the two sisters. "How are things going out at the ranch?" Jack asked, like he gave a damn.

"Fine." She and Rob both snapped the word at the same time, and he cleared his throat and said, "Couldn't be better."

"Ah hell," Joey muttered.

Their sweet teas arrived, and the waitress asked about appetizers. Rob managed to keep his pissed-off demeanor in place the whole time, though it was an effort. They agreed on a couple of sampler platters for the table, and ordered their main courses, and Patty, the new waitress, scurried off looking worried. No wonder...she probably wondered how she'd managed to piss off the boss she'd only just met between drink and appetizer orders.

"I need to use the restroom," Kiley said. She got up, leaving her chair out, and hurried away.

Kendra glanced at her father, and he gave her a very slight nod. "Me too. Excuse me," she said, and she got up and went after her.

Jack pursed his lips, then said, "I can't help but notice things seem...strained between you and my daughter."

"Strained is a good enough word," he said. "But like you said, it's between me and your daughter, so—"

"Sorry, sorry." He held up a hand. "I shouldn't pry."

"You're not splitting up are you?" Joey asked.

Rob sent him a quelling glare.

"But Jeeze, Rob, not now. Not with—"

"That's enough, Joey." He said it firmly.

His brother held his eyes for a minute, then sank back against his chair with a huff and said, "Well this is gonna be a real pleasant evening."

~

Betty Lou Jennings, the real estate agent whose shape roughly matched her beehive, glanced Kiley's way. They were alone in the bathroom, but Kiley held up a finger and nodded toward the door.

Betty Lou nodded in understanding, and Kiley said, "I'm glad I ran into you, Betty Lou. I need a little more time to come up with the money."

"Miz Kellogg, I am out to dinner with my family." Betty Lou always sounded as if she had inhaled a little helium. "If you want to discuss business, call me during business hours. Not that it's going to matter. I told you I was putting your partner's share back on the market, and that's what I'm going to do. It's what he asked me to do, and you don't have any say in it."

"I don't want to lose half of that ranch. I can't lose it. Not now. I just need some time to get the money—"

"You should've thought of that before you tried to swindle a decent, upstanding man like Robby McIntyre."

"He told you?" she asked.

"No details. It must be pretty bad, though, if he's willing to give that place up." Betty Lou lowered her voice to a loud whisper. "Especially given that it's sitting on a potentially lucrative deposit of crude oil."

"He told you about that too?" Kiley gasped.

"Of course he told me. It's a selling point. He's so desperate to get out of this partnership that he's willing to take significantly less than he paid for the place, too."

"How much less?"

Betty Lou smiled evilly, fully into her role. "More than you've got," she said. Then she bustled back into the restaurant.

Kiley turned to the sink and quickly wet her eyes. Then she braced her arms on either side and let her head hang between them.

The door creaked, and Kendra said, "Trouble in paradise?"

She jumped as if startled and shot her sister a look. "None of your business."

Kendra sighed and came closer. "What's going on, Kiley? I thought you two were—how do the cowboys put it? Knockin' boots?"

It had been so much more than that. It had been beautiful, and Rob probably regretted it had ever happened. She'd thoroughly polluted his pure, clean life. Her lips pulled tight and real tears threatened. "You just had to show up, didn't you? After I'd already told him you were dead. How was I supposed to explain that?"

"He can hardly be mad at you for that," she said.

"No. But it made him suspicious. And it didn't take much digging to find out I'd been raised by a con man who was doing time. Then he realized he'd been tricked into buying half the place."

"You tricked him? What did you play?"

"Slippin' Jimmy and Grandma's Rock," she said miserably. Her eyes were honestly burning. "I didn't realize how much I was gonna—" She shook her head, snagged a paper towel and ran it under the faucet, then pressed it to her eyes.

"Gonna what?" Kendra asked, coming closer. "Love him? Do you love him, Kiley?"

"It doesn't matter. He's selling his half. I just...I don't want to lose him."

She wet the towel and dabbed her eyes again, then tried to press them dry with her fingers. "Gotta get back out there. Do I look okay?"

Kendra lifted her hand and pushed Kiley's hair off her forehead. Then she said, "No." And then she opened her purse, took out a compact, and dabbed powder around Kiley's eyes.

Kiley blinked, stunned by how tender she was being. She almost wept again, wishing it could be real.

"I'm sorry if we ruined things for you, Kiley," Kendra said.

She shrugged. "It never would've worked anyway. He's...he's good. He's just good, you know? Way too good for someone like me." She glanced at the mirror, then reached into her purse for a comb, and brushed her hand over the little velvet covered diary. She pulled it out, handed it to Kendra. "I found this at the house. In that hideyhole in the bedroom closet."

Kendra took the tiny book, ran her hand over the velvet. "I don't know if I want to look at it. All my hopes and dreams are in there. All our crazy plans from childhood."

"I don't think it's ever too late to reclaim some of those crazy plans. It's what I'm trying to do."

Kendra held her gaze, and Kiley glimpsed some kind of deep pain behind her sister's eyes. "It's too late for me," she said. "But maybe not for you."

She handed the book back, but Kiley shook her head. "No. Keep it. One of these days, maybe you'll want to remember."

Kendra nodded and dropped the diary into her bag.

Somehow, they got through dinner. Somehow, Rob managed to act pissed off and Kiley managed to act wounded and kind of angry about it, and Joey, who was in on everything, managed to act confused and concerned. Kiley declined dessert and everyone else followed suit, and finally they were able to make their excuses and leave.

She got into the parking lot and looked around for her car. Rob had insisted they drive it there. But it was nowhere in sight.

Rob, however, was heading right toward a little red Jeep Wrangler's passenger door.

"What are you—?"

"Don't smile too hard, they might still be watching," he said. "But this is your new ride."

"Are you freaking kidding me?" She almost grinned then glanced toward the windows, and frowned again.

"Hop in. Keys are above the visor."

She hopped in, flipped the visor, caught the twin keys that slid off it into her lap. She started it up, and it came to life on the first try. "This is the nicest car I've ever had."

"Yeah, well paste your RBF back on and let's get out of here. You look a little too happy."

She sent him a grateful look, put it into reverse to back out of the spot, and didn't dare smile until they hit the road.

"Do you think your family bought it?" he asked.

"Yeah. I do. I was very convincing in the restroom. How about your part? Did you pull it off?"

He nodded. "Joey took me aside and handed me the envelope, said it had been delivered to the saloon. When I checked to be sure your father was within earshot, I found he was taking care of that on his own. You're right, he's nosy as hell. Anyway, the oil company's logo was unmistakable the front. It was very authentic looking."

"Did you say your lines?"

"I did."

"I'm really sorry I missed that." She was truly enjoying herself. The Wrangler drove like a dream. "Will you do it for me now?"

"Aw, come on—"

"Do it just like you did it for Dad. Please?"

He sighed heavily, then nodded. "Okay, but you have to be Joey. Hand me the envelope."

Smiling, she mimed handing him something.

He took the invisible handoff, looked at it, and began. "Another one? How the hell do they find out so fast?"

"Probably bribing someone at the geological surveyor's office," she replied, as Joey had been instructed to do.

"I'm glad it's not my problem anymore."

"You stand to make a lot of money, Rob," Kiley said, again, repeating what would have been Joey's line. "This is the wrong time to sell."

"I already *have* a lot of money. My sanity's worth more." He said it in a low, angry tone. Then smiled and lifted his brows. "Eh?"

Kiley let go of the wheel to applaud, then took hold again in time to pull into their driveway.

"Do you think it'll work?" Rob asked.

"It should. I don't know. I guess we'll see."

He nodded. "I guess we will. In the meantime..." He opened the glove compartment, pulled out a square blue packet, handed it to her.

She looked down at a full set of guitar strings, then up him again, feeling warm all over. "You didn't have to do that. You're too sweet to me, Rob."

"Oh, I've got my own selfish reasons. I'm gonna demand you play for me before the night is out. That's the price of those strings. Take it or leave it."

She nodded. "I'll take it." Twisting the key, she pulled it from the switch, and said, "Thank you, Rob. For...for all of it. For even still being here."

"I'm where I want to be," he told her. "And you're welcome."

# CHAPTER SIXTEEN

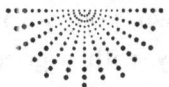

"*I* think I've figured it out," Kiley said.

They were sitting on the sofa, watching *Ancient Aliens*. She wasn't sure why he was watching *Ancient Aliens* at midnight, but she knew why she was. She didn't want to go to bed alone.

She wished she could believe his motives were similar.

"Figured what out?" he asked.

"How to pay back all my...legless Chihuahua donors."

He closed his eyes, either because it was a painful reminder of who she really was and what she'd done, or to avoid smiling at the terminology. She couldn't tell which in the blue glow of the TV screen light. "How?"

"I can get a mortgage. You know, put my half up as collateral, take the lump sum and pay all those legless-chihuahua-donors back. And then just make monthly payments to the bank, like a normal person would."

He sat up straighter and nodded. "That's a pretty good plan."

"Once Holiday Ranch starts making money, I'm gonna start paying back the others, with interest. They won't take as long. I didn't game often, or get very much when I did. Not until this last time. This last time I got...I got everything."

He looked at her, nodded to let her know he understood.

"It's too valuable to me not to pay for it honestly. You know?"

"I know." His heart was filling with her.

"You think I could get approved? For a mortgage?"

"If they turn you down, you can just try again with a co-signer. I know a cowboy with a good credit score who'd be willing to help."

She stared into his eyes and said, "What's gonna happen to us, when this is over? If...if we win, I mean."

He stared right back. "I—"

"No, wait. Don't tell me. There's something more pressing I need to say to you."

He leaned back and said, "Okay."

"Okay," she repeated. "Okay, so, I get that what happened between us was...just what it was. Nothing more. And I get that it doesn't necessarily mean anything. But...but this is gonna end, one way or another, within the next forty eight hours or so." She closed her eyes and rushed on. "And I'd like to spend at least the next few of those hours all wrapped up in you."

A rush of something warm flooded his chest. He saw the uncertainty in her eyes, the honesty—yes, honesty, there. And he said, "Okay."

~

Seven a.m.

The window was open, curtains billowing softly in the sweet summer breeze. Birds were singing like they'd all lost their minds to bliss. And she understood that feeling, because she woke up beside Rob McIntyre, the most amazing human male on the planet. She was spooning in front of him, his arm around her, every inch of them in blissful, naked contact. Kiley tried to imagine this was her real life, that she could wake up every morning just like this. She closed her eyes and made believe she was his, and he was hers. That they slept together every single night, lived together every day. That they might even have kids, someday.

Maybe it could actually happen that way.

Unless she failed. If this game went south and her father carried out his threat to expose her for her crimes, it would be over. And even if Rob forgave her, the town never would. His family never would. Especially not if Jack and Kendra skipped town with so much of their money.

Her eyes popped open and she stared at the wall. Was she making the right call? Should she just turn her family in and let them deal with the consequences of their actions? Was there really any way she could win?

Rob was breathing deep and even. Her cell phone vibrated. She'd turned off the sound, but she could hear it jiggling against the night stand. She slid out from under his arm in slow motion, wriggled her way to the edge of the bed and groped.

There was a text from Betty Lou Jennings: *Your father just called, offered 350k for Rob's half. It's on. 9 am, Cal's office. Pass it on.*

She typed OK, hit send, and watched the message fly, then put the phone down and returned to her happy place, in Rob McIntyre's arms.

He kissed the top of her head. "Who texted?"

"Betty Lou," she told him. "Dad took the bait." She rolled onto her back. "We need to meet in Caleb's office in two hours."

He grinned, then frowned at her. "And yet, you're not dancing for joy or running around to get ready," he said.

"No. Because this might be the last time I get to lie in bed with you. And I'm not ready to end it just yet."

"I'm not either," he said. And then with his eyes all dark and smokey, he kissed her. And then he kept on kissing her and rolled her beneath him in the softness of the bed.

~

As she looked up from the passenger seat of Rob's truck, Kiley saw her father's car across Main Street at the bank. "He's doing it," she whispered. "He's withdrawing all the money he stole from the town."

"Now all we have to do is get him to hand it over," Rob said.

"If he sees me with you, he'll know something's up. This is the crucial part, Rob. Dad's sharp. If anything is the least bit off...."

"I've got this," he told her. "Trust me."

"I'm trying. You're just too damn honest."

"I'm a better liar than you are." He drove around the corner, parked out of sight from the bank, and the two of them got out and went into Caleb's law office, despite the *Closed* sign on the door. They walked through the reception area and directly into a conference room with a long wooden table surrounded by comfortable looking chairs. Caleb got up when Kiley walked in.

Betty Lou Jennings just beamed at her. "It's an amazing thing you're doing for this town, Kiley," she said. Then she quickly schooled her features when the bell over the door chimed.

Caleb nodded toward a door at the back of the room, and Kiley slipped through it. It led directly to his office, and when she looked around, she realized his computer was showing a live feed of everything happening in the room next door. She could watch, and maybe even listen in. Taking a seat in the oversized leather chair behind the desk, Kiley spotted a headset and put it on, staring at the large monitor.

Rob and Caleb were still standing when her father and Kendra walked in.

Kendra looked nervous, was checking around, examining corners, looking out windows.

Dammit, she knew something was up.

"Welcome, Mr. Kellogg, Miss Kellogg. I'm Caleb Caine Montgomery, and I'm here to make sure everything is legal and above board. I'm working for Betty Lou Jennings, so that makes me a neutral third party between the buyer and the seller. Is that acceptable to both of you?"

Jack pursed his lips and said, "I'll let you know."

"Also, full disclosure, we're all being recorded." Caleb nodded toward the camera mounted in an upper corner. "That's standard. I like to have video to refer back to. There are coffee and scones from Sunny's Bakery," he added with a nod toward the table against the far wall. "Help yourselves and we'll get on with things."

Rob went to the table, grabbed a cup of coffee and a scone, but didn't take a bite or a sip. Jack was watching him like a hawk.

"Well now," Betty Lou said, from the conference table. She already had a luscious looking scone on a plate in front of her, or rather half of one. Kiley wished she'd have had time to grab one herself. "This should be a pretty simple transaction. I have the agreement right here." She pulled a thick document out of a folder that had been lying on the table in front of her. "This is the purchase agreement. I'll mark it paid in full as soon as your check has cleared."

She pushed the documents across the table to Kiley's father, who put on his bifocals and leaned back in his seat to peruse them.

Kiley knew that opening page by heart. Her father was purchasing said tract of land, tax map number 14.1.6.5.1-99, for the price of three-hundred-fifty thousand dollars on this date and at this time.

"You'll also need to sign this." She slid another document toward him, sending a shy smile with it.

"And what is this?" Jack asked. His brows had risen a notch. He was sensing something.

*Just sign it,* Kiley willed in silence. *Just sign it and get out of my life.*

Caleb said, "It states that you are giving sole decision-making authority as to the uses, disposal of, and exploitation of rights of the property, to your daughter, Kiley Kellogg."

"I don't believe that was part of my offer," Jack said, shooting a look at Rob.

Rob got up. "I know, and I apologize, but it's part of my counter offer, and it's a deal breaker," he said. "I'm betraying her by selling to you. The least I can do is make sure you're never more than a silent partner." He shrugged. "Besides, do you really care?"

"I only care that I receive my share of the profits...should there be any." He smiled vaguely, then lowered his head and kept reading. He read and read. He flipped a page, then flipped back, then flipped it again.

"Did you bring payment?" Caleb asked.

"I did." Jack pulled a cashier's check from his pocket and laid it on the table.

In the next room, Kiley held her breath. And then Jack said, "Who has a pen?"

Rob, Caleb, and Betty Lou all whipped out pens at once.

Jack lifted his brows, narrowed his eyes. Suspicion was fully awake behind them. Kiley knew that look and her heart sank. He smelled a con. There was no way he'd go through with it now.

"Dad," Kendra said. She was still standing in the doorway, and she nodded toward the front of the reception area. "That guy is back. I'm telling you, I think he's a Fed."

"I'm obligated to report crimes or intended ones," Caleb said. "I wouldn't say too much more than that in my presence."

"I *told you* he was following me," Kendra went on, ignoring Caleb as if he hadn't spoken.

Jack got up and looked where she was staring. "Hell, Kendra."

Kiley jumped to her feet, her heart in her throat. Her sister had faked her own death. Her father was an ex-con on probation. And some kind of federal law enforcer was parked outside. They'd both end up in prison unless she did something. She went to the office door and opened it, but her eyes were still on the computer.

Kendra said, "Will you just sign, Dad, so we can get out of here?"

Jack looked past his daughter and apparently, saw Kendra's pursuer. Kiley couldn't see the road from Caleb's office. Her father nodded grimly. Then he went back to the table, scribbled his name across both documents, and then signed the check. "Send a copy of the paperwork here." He scribbled an address on a notepad and shoved it across the table. "Where's the back door?"

"Around to the right," Caleb said.

Jack nodded, then took hold of Kendra's shoulders. "Wait here. Stay out of sight. I'll pull the car around back." Then he released her and headed out of the conference room. Kiley turned to watch him stride through the reception area, through the slightly open door.

The second he was outside, she burst out of the office and grabbed Kendra's hand just as she came out of the conference room. "Come on." She tugged her through the reception area, around the corner to the back door, pushed it open.

But her sister planted her feet.

"Go on, Kendra," Kiley said. "I'll go out front and distract the cop. Let him think I'm you, give you time to get away." As she spoke she glanced toward the front door in case anyone was coming. But all she saw was Dax Russell sitting out front in his pimped-out Charger. He gave her a nod.

Frowning, she looked back at her sister. "But...but that's—"

"He's a great guy. I owe him a lot. When I asked him to follow me around the past two days, he didn't even argue."

"But...but why?"

"Had a feeling I might need to rush Dad out of town. But mostly, to help my sister get the life she deserves."

"You mean...you knew?"

She made a face. "Pssh. Of course I knew. I can always tell when you're lying, Kiley." Then she shrugged. "You're not entirely hopeless at the game after all, are you? I mean, Dad didn't really just buy Rob's share of the ranch. Did he?"

"No. He bought that land he was pretending to raise money to buy, just as promised, for a reservoir project for the town."

"And he gave you the power to do whatever you want with it." She nodded when Kiley said nothing. "Maybe there's hope for you yet. You just conned the best grifter in the business."

"If he was the best, then why did he fall for it? You didn't."

Kendra nodded. "He was about to catch on, Kiley. I had to play the Dax card." She put her hands on Kiley's shoulders. "Always have a Plan B, Sis. Always have an exit strategy." Kiley nodded. Then Kendra said, "He's gonna be pissed. But I don't think he'll turn you in for The Legless Chihuahua. If he seems like he's going to, I think I can talk him out of it."

"I'll have every donor paid back by the time he figures out what happened. You tell him that. I'll be a productive and beloved Big Falls resident by then. I'll have prevented the entire town from being robbed by then, too. Don't think for a minute Betty Lou isn't gonna tell this story. I'd get a slap on the wrist."

"Wouldn't be worth his effort," Kendra said. "You did good, Sis."

A sob caught in Kiley's throat and she hugged her sister. "I love you, Kendra. I'll make sure Betty Lou keeps your name out of it."

"Thanks. I love you too." In the distance, a horn blew. They pulled apart. "I'll call when we get somewhere, okay?"

"You better."

Kendra turned and went outside. She got in the passenger door and the car sped away in a haze of red Oklahoma dust.

Kiley stood there, staring at the dark cloud her family had left behind. Her father would never forgive her once he realized he'd been duped. He'd been starting to get suspicious, would have thought to double check the tax map number if he'd had a few more minutes. But Kendra had played the Dax card, as she'd put it. Kendra had helped her to do the right thing.

"You okay, babe?" Rob asked.

She turned around. It registered on her that he wasn't alone, but she didn't care, because he opened his arms and she fell right into them. "We did it," he whispered. "We actually did it."

Betty Lou and Caleb were standing behind him. Over his shoulder, Kiley saw Dax driving away.

"Well, there's just one more order of business," Betty Lou said. And turning, she all but skipped back into the conference room. Everyone followed, and she quickly slid another document in front of Kiley. "Sign here to sell the property your father just purchased, to the town of Big Falls Oklahoma for the sum of one dollar. Everything's exactly as you asked," she said softly.

Everyone in the room was looking at her. And not the way she used to feel people looked at her. Not judging or condemning or mistrusting. But kind, loving, and kind of admiring.

She had to blink away tears to see where to sign and as she scratched her name on the dotted line, one of them fell from her cheek and blended with the ink.

~

Kiley and Rob sat on the riverbank, under the biggest full moon she thought she'd ever seen. It painted the river in white that glittered like a Kincaid painting. They'd spread a blanket on the grass and the boulder was their backrest. She strummed her guitar and sang *Sunshine on My Shoulders*, but substituted *Moonshine* instead.

When she finished, Rob said, "That was amazing. You have to play at The Long Branch."

She blushed and set the guitar aside.

"It was pretty cool, what your sister did. What Dax did, too, considering."

"I think he'd do anything she asked him to. I think he's still in love with her."

Kiley took a deep breath, leaned back against the boulder and said, "I think I've done everything I need to do here, Rob. I proved to myself that I could be a good person. That I could do the right thing. And Mrs. Terwilliger called today. The bank is happy to approve my mortgage. I just have to go in tomorrow to finalize everything. But if you want to buy me out of my half of the ranch, I'll sell to you, instead. I can pay those people back either way. I understand if you don't want to be in business with me. A guy as honest as you—"

He pressed a finger to her lips and stared into her eyes. "I love you." Her eyes widened. "And no matter what you do or what you've done, I'm still gonna love you."

"How... do you know?"

"Cause I tried not to love you already." He shrugged. "A couple of times. Didn't work. Still love you. Doesn't seem like I have any choice in the matter, and if I did, I think I'd choose to keep on loving you anyway."

She let those words sink in, then suddenly leaned up and kissed his mouth over and over, talking in between . "I love you...too. It's the biggest thing... I've ever felt. And it keeps... getting bigger... all the time."

"It's good we...both feel the same." Then he shoved his hand into his jeans pocket. Her head was angled across his chest so she saw it. When it came out, it came out with a ring. Its gold and breathtaking diamond winked in the moonlight.

She sucked in a sharp breath and stared at him, stunned. "Robby!" And then, "*Robby?*"

He got up and pulled her to her feet. Once she was standing, he took her hand and dropped down onto one knee. "Kiley Louise Kellogg, I want us to be partners in everything, not just in Holiday Ranch. I want to fall asleep and wake up with you in my arms every night and day for the rest of my life. What do you say?"

She stared down into his eyes and felt the strangest sensation she had ever experienced. She realized that she was living the very moment when all her dreams were coming true. It was surreal.

"I say yes," she said. She tugged him until he stood up, then stood on tiptoe and whispered against his lips. "Oh, Rob, we're gonna be so happy."

"Gonna be? Nah. We're already there," he said.

And then he kissed her and she knew that her brand new life had finally, truly begun.

–The End–

**Continue reading for an excerpt from book 3 in
the McIntyre Men series,
Oklahoma Starshine.**

# PREVIEW OKLAHOMA
## STARSHINE

# CHAPTER ONE

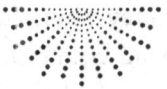

## CHAPTER 1

*Y*ou wouldn't have known it to look at him, with three soused cowgirls hanging from his arms, but Joey McIntyre was bored. And charming these ladies into letting him drive them home was nothing more than his duty as part owner of the Long Branch, Big Falls Oklahoma's most popular claim to fame, after the falls themselves. This year, though, the nearby Holiday Ranch was rapidly becoming another.

The player piano was tinkling an 1890s version of "Joy to the World," and hidden projectors beamed tiny illuminated images on every wall; Christmas trees, Santas and stars.

A soft-handed sweetie stroked his face, or tried to, and managed to poke him in the eye. "You're a real hero, giving us a ride home, Joey. You gonna come in for a nightcap?" Her knees bent and she sank floorward. Joe tightened his arm around her waist to hold her upright, and she beamed up at him, wafting beer breath that would've scared the jingle bells off a reindeer at twenty paces.

"Yeah, Joe, you have to come in," said the one on the other

side. She was trying to make herself tall enough to nuzzle his neck, but kept tipping off her stilettos.

The girls' night out had taken a turn for the rowdy by the fifth or so round, and when one of the girls reached for her keys, Joey knew it was time to step in. It was times like these he wished Darryl Champlain hadn't quit his job as their bouncer-slash-head of security to go back to full-time songwriting.

The third hayseed honey shuffled along behind him, her hands on his shoulders, head kind of bouncing along against his back because she could hardly hold it upright. She mumbled something but he wasn't sure what.

They all wore skin-tight jeans so low slung they gave even scrawny girls a muffin top, and blouses that showed varying amounts of cleavage.

"I should've cut them off," the new waitress said. "I should've cut them off at four rounds." Her name was Heidi, and it fit. Blond hair and blue eyes so round she always looked either scared or surprised.

"I think they had a head start before they got here," Joey said. He didn't want her to think she was in trouble. "It's a bar. People are gonna drink. Will you check to see if we got all their crap from the table?"

Nodding and gnawing her lip, Heidi hurried away. One of the girls listed left, taking him and the other two with her, but he managed to keep from hitting the floor, then got them all upright and back on track for the garland-draped batwing doors again.

He looked back at the bar, not wanting to leave the place unattended, but as usual, his brother Jason was nowhere to be found. He was spending all his time at his fixer-upper outside of town or over at Sunny's Bakery these days. Not much help running the saloon anymore. But he did spot Rob, taking a shift behind the bar while his country-fresh Kiley sat on a saddle shaped barstool, making doe eyes at him.

He caught Rob's eye, inclined his head, and his brother hopped over the bar and jogged up to him. "You uh, sure do have your hands full there, little brother."

"Yeah. Can you hold down the fort while I get them home?"

"I can." He assisted by taking Joey's keys from his belt loop, and putting them into one of his hands, which he couldn't move because it was holding up a drunk girl. A drunk girl who was smiling sloppily up at him and trying to bat her lashes. Looked more like she had something in her eyes. "You gonna be okay with all this?" Rob asked.

"Lucy's place is the closest. I'll drop 'em off there, make sure they get inside."

"And not go inside with them. Cause they're drunk."

Joey sent him a look. "You think I'm immoral or just stupid?"

Rob shrugged. "Hey, you're the billionaire bachelor of Big Falls, pal. I'm just looking out for you." He eyed the women, each of whom was pawing Joey in her own way. Suzy Jennings, Betty Lou's niece, was petting his back like he was a cat. Geri Starbuck (no relation) was trying to lick his neck, but couldn't reach.

"Just help me get 'em in the truck, huh, Rob?"

Nodding, Rob turned toward the exit, just as a redhead came through the batwing doors, stopped about three feet in front of Joey and looked him right in the eyes.

He was so surprised to see her that he let go of the girls on either side of him, and took a step toward her. All three cowgirls landed ass first on the hardwood floor.

"You dropped something," she said with a sarcastic lift of one brow.

"Emily?"

"Hello Joe. Haven't changed much, I see."

"I don't know what you...oh, this? No, this isn't what you... Shoot, how the hell are you? It's been what, four years?"

"Something like that."

Rob cleared his throat and Joey remembered his brother's presence, looked his way, saw him nod at the three on the floor as if to remind him of his unfinished business. But Rob's new bride stepped in. "Rob and I will get these three home so you can catch up with your...friend." Then she extended her hand. "Kiley McIntyre. Welcome to Big Falls."

Emily smiled, her face softening. She was still beautiful. More elegant than he remembered. Her cheekbones seemed more pronounced, her eyes, more deeply set than before. Then again, she'd only been twenty last time he'd seen her.....

Outside his father's Texas mansion, in the grotto behind the waterfall, among the ferns and honeysuckle, beneath a midsummer moon.

"Emily Hawkins," she said. "Good to meet you, Kiley." Then she added, "Hello Rob."

"Good to see you again, Em. How are you?"

"Great. Wonderful." Joey thought her eyes didn't match her words, and while her lips tried to turn themselves upward, it wasn't a smile. It was some kind of hidden pain, trying to impersonate one.

Kiley helped the girls to their feet, one at a time. "You're gonna ride in the back of the pickup. You're gonna sit still and shut up and hold your vomit until we get you home. Understood?"

They nodded at her, and no wonder. She was sweet and young and freckled, but she sounded more like Vidalia just then.

"You puke in the truck, you're cleaning it with your toothbrushes. So just don't." She took a girl's arm in each hand and marched them out the door. The third was clawing at Joey's jeans, trying to pull herself to her feet.

Rob grabbed her under her arms and hauled her upright, then steered her toward the door. "Come on, let's go." He sent Emily a nod, glanced at Joe and said, "I'll be back to help you close up."

He nodded, but wasn't really paying attention. They all got out into the parking lot, and the place went quieter. Patrons stopped muttering about the spectacle and went back to their own drinks and conversations.

For a minute he and Emily just stood there, staring at each other, and he felt the years fall away. He felt like they were kids again, all wrapped up in each other, hearts pounding with the all-consuming power of young love.

She blushed, then she seemed to tear her eyes off him, taking a slow look around the saloon. "So you're a bar owner now."

"Part owner, with Jason, Rob and Dad. Lately, though, it's mostly just me."

"Whole family's in town, then?"

"Mom's still in Texas. She got the place in the divorce. Remarried. She's pretty happy."

"Who wouldn't be?"

Was her tone sharper just then? "Come on in, I'll show you around." He put a hand on her arm, and she shied away from it, but walked further inside.

"You serve food, too?" she asked.

He nodded and walked her between the pulled-back, red velvet curtains that marked out the border between barroom and dining room. An evergreen tree took up about four tables worth of space near the front windows, but it was worth it. It bore only twinkling multi-colored lights, at the moment, and filled the whole place with that pine-scented holiday feeling. The ornaments would come later.

"We've got a chef that'll make you weep," he said, walking her slowly around the dining room. The chairs were already up on top of the tables. "It's really a touristy kind of place. We have dinner theater, bad guys and saloon girls, fake shoot-outs and poker games gone bad." He nodded toward the source of the happy holiday music. "That's an original player piano. Dad had it restored."

"Cute," she said, but the tone didn't match the word.

He looked at her face to see her expression and got stuck on her eyes. Emily's eyes had always been impenetrable, as dark green and shiny as wet lily pads. And they still were. "So the tourists don't mind the alcoholic cowgirl hookers?"

He frowned at her and wondered if life had turned her mean. "They're not so bad, Em. Just some local girls, best friends their whole lives. Lucy's getting married next weekend. I think tonight was a pre-bachelorette party bachelorette party." He looked toward the big front windows, the parts not blocked by evergreen boughs, and said, "Tell you the truth, I think it was good for her to let off some steam. Wedding planning is stressful."

"I wouldn't know," she said, which made him dart a quick look at her ring finger, left hand. Bare as ever. Why did that send a surge of knee-weakening relief through him?

"I would." He said it just to see her reaction, which was to look down real fast, and catch her bottom lip between her teeth. "Robby just married Kiley in September. I thought the Brand gals would kill each other before—"

"Brand gals?"

He pulled a couple of chairs off a table, set them upright. "Dad married Vidalia Brand, mother of five remarkable females. Turns out Vidalia was his first love, and one of Vidalia's daughters is his."

"You have a sister?" she asked, sitting down and widening her eyes at the same time. Why did the question seem disproportionately important?

"That I do. Her name's Selene." He hadn't sat down yet. "You want a drink, or something to eat? Ned's gone home, but there are always snacks around."

She crossed one leg over the other. Her jeans hugged her calves, then vanished into the tops of fake fur boots, all the rage with the local girls. "How's your coffee?"

"Best in town." He shrugged. "Well, next to Sunny's." He went to the curtain, leaned into the barroom and caught Heidi's eye. "Bring us a pot of coffee?"

"Sure, boss."

"You okay out here for a few minutes?" he went on, giving the barroom a quick scan. Only about a dozen folks remained, half of them playing cards, the others looking pretty docile and content.

"If I can't, I'll holler," she said.

He nodded and took his seat at the little round table for two. He could barely believe Emily was actually here. "I looked for you at your dad's funeral," he said. "We all did. Henry was...well he was like family to us. We loved him, you know."

"I saw you there," she said. Then she shrugged. "I just couldn't handle...people, you know? So I stayed out of sight until everyone else left. Said my goodbyes in private."

"It was a little more than that, though," he said slowly. "You didn't even call. Some stranger came by to tell us what happened. I rushed over to check on you, and you were just gone. I called and called—"

"I know."

"I was worried about you. Which, given the self-centered jerk I used to be, is saying something."

"Used to be?" she muttered, half under her breath. She wasn't looking him in the eye.

"Sorry, that's not the answer we were looking for. The correct response was, 'Aw, you weren't all that bad.' " He was joking.

But Em didn't so much as crack a smile. There was something in her eyes, something big, and dark and inexpressibly sad. He reached across the table, laid his hand on top of hers. She jerked a little, like she wanted to pull it away, but then stilled again and just let her hand rest there, all stiff and twitchy and cold.

"What brings you to Big Falls, Emily?"

"What brought *you* here?" It was delivered as quick as an Ali counterpunch.

Just then, Heidi came in with a tray and unloaded it onto the table between them. Then she poured from the big brown earthenware coffeepot, filling two man-sized mugs with longhorn skull logos.

"Thanks, Heidi."

"No problem." She set the coffeepot on the table, between the matching cream and sugar holders. Then she took a lighter from her apron pocket and lit the candle inside its cactus-shaped globe made of green tinted glass. When she left, she freed the red velvet curtains from their tie backs. They fell together, silent as snow, muting the sounds from the barroom and leaving them in complete privacy.

"Where were we?" he asked.

"You were telling me why you moved here."

"Right. Well, long story short, Dad got sick. We thought we were gonna lose him. He came here to see the love of his life one last time and to build the Long Branch. I think it was supposed to be a legacy for Jason, Rob and me."

"He's okay, though?" she asked.

Joe nodded. "Wound up finding a daughter he never knew he had and a cure he never even expected." He gazed past her briefly. "It was kind of miraculous the way it all went down. Christmastime and all."

Emily stopped with her coffee mug halfway to her lips, blinked three times, rapidly, then seemed to steady herself and took a sip. "That *is* good coffee," she said. "So you came for your dad and just never left?"

"There's something about this town," Joey said, gazing again toward the windows. "You'll feel it, too, if you stay around here long enough. How long did you say you're here for?"

"I didn't," she said.

He frowned at her, wondered why she was being so secretive. "Did you ever become a vet, like you always planned?"

"You remember that."

"I remember everything." Especially the night he'd caught her and her girlfriends using his father's pool. They'd climbed the fence and sneaked in. He'd heard the splashing, gone out to investigate, and there she'd been. Emily, in a bikini, looking like a young man's dream come true. He remembered the way the water was all beaded on her smooth skin, and the way the pool lights lit up her dark green eyes, and how he forgot his aquaphobia for a few seconds while he was staring at her.

He was staring again. She was staring back, but she seemed to realize it and tugged her eyes away. "I did, actually," she said, and her words jarred him out of the memory.

It took him a minute to remember his question. Oh, the vet thing. And then her answer lit up in his brain and he said, "You did? That's great, Em! So do you work for a clinic or—?"

"I have my own practice." she said.

He sat back in his seat, blinking at her, impressed to his core. "Hell, I don't know why I'm surprised. Everyone always knew you'd do amazing things with your life. Graduated high school early and already had an associate's degree."

"All those college classes they offer in high school these days. It's not that hard."

"You had your BA at eighteen. That's hard. You must've sped through vet school at the speed of light, too."

She shrugged, lowered her eyes a little.

"So where is it? Your practice?" He would love to see where she worked, he thought. To see what she'd built, what she'd done since with her life he'd seen her.

But more than that, he wanted to know why she'd left him.

"Anywhere I want." She leaned back in her seat, and for the

first time, seemed to relax a little bit. Sipping her coffee, clearly enjoying it, she went on. "It's a mobile practice. I have this tricked-out van with everything I need inside. I call it the VetMobile."

The way she said it, it rhymed with Batmobile, and he got it immediately, and grinned. "Do your patients shine a spotlight into the night sky when they need you?"

"Yeah, with a vet-shaped silhouette in it."

"Va-va-voom, woman. If it's shaped like *this* vet, it's gonna be a very confusing signal." She rolled her eyes at his flattery, but he went right on. "Men will flock to the light, only to find..." He left it unfinished, to let her fill in the blanks.

She shrugged. "Anything from a mare about to foal to a constipated guinea pig."

"That's not a real case," he said.

She lifted her brows and nodded, and he slapped his thigh and laughed. "That's great, Emily. That's really amazing. You did your father proud."

Her smile died. "I like to think so."

"So where's your territory? Where is home for you these days?"

"I've been in New Mexico for a while. I like it there."

He nodded. "I've been there. Beautiful country."

"It is. But it's never felt like home to me." She sat up a little straighter again. "This saloon ownership agrees with you, doesn't it Joey?"

He looked around the place, realized he was proud of it. "It does. Jason and Rob are both pulling out, bit by bit. They've got their own irons in the fire, and this isn't their passion. Rob married Kiley, and they bought a ranch together. He raises Thoroughbreds and she caters to the local kids with special events for every holiday. Dad wants to retire, show his feisty bride the world. So I'm taking on more and more around here."

"And you resent it," she guessed.

He flinched when she said that, but had to admit, that was the guy he used to be. "I expected to resent it, when I first realized what was happening, but I don't. I really don't. I kind of like it, as a matter of fact. Lately, I keep getting ideas to expand the place, make it better." He shrugged. "Who'd have thought?"

"Yeah, who'd have thought." She looked at him a little oddly for a long moment, and then quickly glanced at her phone. "God, we've been talking for an hour. I've gotta go." She rose, slugged the rest of her coffee back and put the cup down.

He got up, too. "Coffee's on the house," he said.

"I pay my own way, Joey." She fished a couple of singles out of her jeans and put them on the table. "It was...it was good to see you again."

"It was fantastic to see you," he said, feeling almost desperate. She couldn't just leave. "Are you um...do you have a room somewhere? I've got the whole second floor, if you need—"

"No, I'm good." She looked up at him, paused, nodded as if she'd made a decision. "I'm staying at the B and B."

"B and B?"

"Yeah, um, Peabody's? Out on Church Road?"

"Oh, the boarding house. Ida Mae's place." His spine sort of dissolved in relief. She wasn't leaving...yet. "Okay, good. I'm glad you're...sticking around for a while."

She nodded. "So...yeah. I'll probably, you know, see you."

"Yeah, you will," he said.

He was holding open the curtain by then, and she turned and walked across the bar, through the batwing doors and then right out the bigger doors to the outside.

Joey resisted the urge to jump up and click his heels. Hot damn, Emily Hawkins, right here in Big Falls.

All of the sudden, Joey McIntyre was the furthest thing from bored.

~

Joey McIntyre hadn't changed a bit.

That was what she'd thought when she'd walked into the tacky cowboy saloon. Hot hometown honeys dripping from him like a rich widow's jewelry. He'd always been a player. She oughtta know, he'd played her like a fiddle.

A willing, stupid, naive, starry-eyed fiddle. Yeah, that. Until he drove the bow right through her heart.

"Doesn't matter." She walked up to her van and unlocked it with the key fob. As always, before she got in, she took a second to love the thing. It was glossy black with dark burgundy swooshes. And there was a very Bat-signal-like logo on it, unless you looked close enough to notice it was a winged-V in a white oval. White lettering followed the curve, proclaiming it The VetMobile. She opened the door and got in, running a hand over the two-tone "pleather" seats that matched the paint job. Even the car seat in the back matched. You know, underneath its layer of crust, composed of Goldfish crumbs and apple juice.

There was no reason, she told herself, to believe was anything but what he'd always been—a spoiled, rich, self-centered playboy who didn't have a care in the world for anybody but himself. Worse yet, he liked it that way.

She imagined his face when he'd first looked at her. God, he was still just as beautiful to her as he'd always been. The tall lanky frame, those long arms that used to wrap all the way around her and then some. And his sweet face, and chocolate brown eyes and little boy lashes. God she loved looking at that face of his. Always had.

That face could charm the moon out of the sky.

She started the van, flipped on the headlights, and then the heater. It was chilly tonight. And then she backed carefully out of the gaudy saloon's parking lot and headed back onto the winding, narrow road. It turned into Main Street once it hit the village. She didn't have to go that far, though, hanging a right onto Church Street, and then past the church little white church with the big red doors, and on up to the B and B—make that boarding house—where she was staying.

It was a pretty Victorian in a violet shade so subtle it seemed white at nighttime, and its elaborate trim work was decked out in pine green, minty pink, and baby blue. The sign that swung from a wrought iron holder had matching wood-trimmed edges, all scrolled like the trim on the house, and read Peabody's Boarding House. Ida Mae Peabody's holiday decorations were far more understated than most of the others in Big Falls. She had a single white electric candle in each window and a giant wreath on the front door. Period.

Emily shut off the van and hopped out. The front door swung open before she even reached it, and Ida Mae herself stood there, holding a cherub with burnt gold curls on her hip. But the angel quickly wriggled free and ran toward the porch steps. Emily reached them first, and scooped her up before she could fall.

Matilda didn't even notice her brush with disaster.

"You're supposed to be asleep, young lady!" Emily said, closing her eyes and just inhaling the smell of Tilda's hair. The greatest smell in the known universe.

"I waked up!" Matilda said.

"I'm sorry I wasn't there. I had to see someone."

"Was it Santa?"

"No, honey. It wasn't Santa."

Matilda pouted. "But we have to find him and tell him so he'll be able to find me!"

"And we will. I promise."

"Tomorrow?" Tilda asked.

"Yes," she promised. "Tomorrow."

Tilda hugged Emily's neck a little tighter. "I love you, Mommy."

"I love you, too, baby."

## Oklahoma Starshine

# ALSO AVAILABLE

**The McIntyre Men**
Oklahoma Christmas Blues
Oklahoma Moonshine
Oklahoma Starshine
Shine On Oklahoma
Baby By Christmas
Oklahoma Sunshine

**The Oklahoma Brands**
The Brands who Came for Christmas
Brand-New Heartache
Secrets and Lies
A Mommy For Christmas
One Magic Summer
Sweet Vidalia Brand

# ABOUT THE AUTHOR

*New York Times* and *USA Today* bestselling novelist Maggie Shayne has published sixty-two novels and twenty-two novellas for five major publishers over the course of twenty-two years. She also spent a year writing for American daytime TV dramas *The Guiding Light* and *As the World Turns*, and was offered the position of co-head writer of the former; a million-dollar offer she tearfully turned down. It was scary, turning down an offer that big. But her heart was in her books, and she'd found it impossible to do both.

In March 2014, she did something even scarier. She left the world's largest publisher and went "indie."

Now, she is embarking on an exciting new leg of her publishing journey, with most of her titles moving to small press publisher, Oliver Heber Books.

Maggie writes small town contemporary romances like the recent *Bliss in Big Falls* series, which boasts "a miracle in every story."

She cut her teeth on western themed category romances like her classic 90s and early 2000s *The Texas Brand* and *The Oklahoma All-Girl Brands,* and later expanded into romantic suspense and thrillers like *The Secrets of Shadow Falls* and *The Brown and de Luca Novels.*

She is perhaps best known for her beloved paranormal romances, like the brand new *Fatal series* and perennial favorites *The Immortals,* the *By Magic series,* and *Wings in the Night.*

Maggie is a fifteen-time RITA® Award nominee and one-time winner. She lives in the rolling green and forested hilltops of Cortland County NY, wine & dairy country, despite having sworn off both. She is a vegan Wiccan hippy living her best life with her beloved husband Lance, and usually at least two dogs.

Maggie also writes spiritual self-help and runs an online magic shop, BlissBlog.org

Visit Maggie at www.maggieshayne.com